Entangled Hearts

Love's Second Chance

Sarmed Shafi

Dedication

"To the dreamers who dare to love,

In the vast landscape of existence, where the winds of uncertainty blow and the paths of destiny intertwine, this book is dedicated to those who courageously embark on the journey of love. To you, who understand that love is not just a fleeting emotion but a profound force that shapes our lives, this dedication extends with the deepest of sentiments.

Within these pages lie tales woven with threads of passion, longing, and the undying hope that accompanies the pursuit of love. To each reader who turns these pages, I offer you a tribute to the beauty and complexity of human connection.

To the ones who have loved and lost, who have felt the sting of heartbreak and yet continue to believe in the magic of love's embrace, this dedication echoes with empathy and understanding. May these words serve as a balm to your soul, a reminder that every tear shed in the name of love is a testament to its enduring power."

With profound gratitude and boundless affection,

Sarmed Shafi

Acknowledgment

I am deeply grateful to everyone who has contributed to the realization of this book, directly or indirectly. To my family, whose unwavering love and support have sustained me through every twist and turn of this journey, thank you for believing in me even when I doubted myself.

To my friends, who provided encouragement, laughter, and invaluable feedback along the way, your presence in my life is a constant source of inspiration.

A heartfelt thank you goes to my editor and publishing team for their expertise, guidance, and patience throughout the writing and editing process. Your dedication to this project has helped shape it into the best possible version.

I am also indebted to the countless authors whose works have fueled my imagination and taught me the power of storytelling. Your words have left an indelible mark on my heart and mind.

Last but certainly not least, to the readers who will embark on this journey with me, thank you for your curiosity, time, and willingness to immerse yourselves in the world I've created. It is my sincere hope that this story brings you as much joy in reading it as it has brought me in writing it."

With deepest gratitude,

Sarmed Shafi

About the Author

I was born in 1987 and grew up in upstate New York in a small town named Monticello.

As a kid and even as a teenager, I had a problem focusing on books and reading. My go-to line was always that I'd wait for the movie to come out. It wasn't until 2017, driving an hour to work and working 10-hour days, that the radio and Pandora got way too repetitive, and no matter what station I listened to, I would hear the same set of songs over and over. I decided to give audiobooks a try, and I was hooked. It was like a movie was playing in my head, and the books came to life. I picked books based on length because I hoped for a book to last me one workweek. I listened to everything from thrillers to sci-fi, dystopian, and even romance.

I have listened to over 500 books over the course of the last seven years, and I have certainly found some favorite authors. So, why did I decide to write a book?

Well, this wasn't my first book, but it was the easiest to get out of my head. While listening to all the authors and books, my mind would always play what-if scenarios in my head, and I decided to write them down. While working on my main book, I wanted to write these characters kept popping up in my mind, and I decided to let their story out.

Preface

Welcome to the story of two young souls whose paths diverge after college, only to intertwine once more in a serendipitous reunion. In this heartfelt tale, we delve into the lives of Emma, a gifted graphic designer, and Liam, a prosperous architect yearning for deeper connections.

Their story begins at a college reunion, where old memories awaken, reigniting a connection that time failed to extinguish. Set against this backdrop, Emma and Liam begin a journey fraught with emotions and uncertainties yet brimming with the possibility of love's rekindling.

As they navigate through life's trials and triumphs, Emma and Liam confront external challenges, wrestle with their inner doubts, and make heartfelt sacrifices for the sake of their budding relationship. However, be warned, for this tale is laced with unexpected twists. Just as their love reaches its zenith, a startling revelation threatens to upend everything they hold dear.

As you immerse yourself in the pages of this book, prepare to enjoy a voyage infused with reminiscences, fervor, and the complexities of love. So, turn the page now and allow their story to resonate within the depths of your own heart.

Contents

Chapter 1: A Reunion of Hearts

Standing outside the venue of the much-anticipated reunion, Emma took a moment to absorb the familiar sights and sounds that surrounded the college building. The soft rustle of leaves overhead, the distant murmur of students, and the gentle breeze that carried the scent of nostalgia all reminded her of the great time she had spent there.

As she approached the entrance, a chain of memories started flashing across her mind like a montage of moments frozen in time. The imposing college gate, once a symbol of uncertainty and new beginnings, now stood before her as a portal to the past. Emma could not help but recall the nervousness that gripped her the day she entered through the same door for the first time. Back then, the unknown stretched before her like an unexplored landscape.

Almost five years had elapsed since she graduated, donned the cap and gown, and bid farewell to this place. Now, with each step closer, she found herself once again staring at the college gate, a silent witness to the passage of time and a keeper of countless stories. The faded paint on the wrought iron gate hinted at the wear and tear of years gone by, but the memories etched in the grooves of Emma's mind remained vivid and untouched.

She marveled at how the courtyard, once a teeming hub of hurried footsteps and animated chatter, now echoed with a different resonance. The brick pathway beneath her feet felt familiar, almost like retracing the steps of her younger self. As she passed the rows of benches where friendships were forged and secrets were shared, Emma could not help but smile at the simplicity of those moments.

The college building loomed ahead; its grand facade weathered by the seasons but still standing strong. Emma paused to take in the intricate details of the architecture - the arched windows that witnessed countless lectures, the ivy-covered walls that seemed to embrace the building with a touch of nature, and the imposing clock tower that marked the passage of time with each solemn chime.

The excitement within Emma grew with each passing moment. She could almost hear the echoes of laughter and feel the amity that once filled the hallways. The nervousness she felt on that first day had transformed into a warm and fuzzy feeling, like reuniting with an old friend. The college, once a maze of unfamiliar corridors, now seemed like a treasure trove of cherished memories waiting to be revisited.

As Emma reached for the ornate door handle, she drew in a steadying breath, preparing herself to traverse the corridors of time. A momentary hesitation lingered, prompting her to steal a glance at her reflection against the polished glass door. Its drop-shoulder design, draped in a flowing black silk gown, accentuated her every graceful movement. The gown, a symphony of elegance, embraced her form in all the right places, transforming her already sleek physique into something truly enchanting.

Her auburn locks were artfully pulled into a delicate bun, with a few rebellious strands playfully framing her face. Dark, expressive eyes, adorned with a touch of black smokey makeup and layers of mascara, peered back at her reflection. The interplay of her hair and makeup harmonized seamlessly, creating a captivating allure.

Satisfied with the image staring back at her, Emma turned the handle, unlocking the door to the past. The reunion was waiting for her, and so were some old faces. She entered the elegantly decorated hall where the reunion was in full swing. The room was adorned with banners displaying the graduating year, and the walls echoed with the music that bridged the gap between the past and the present.

The atmosphere was a curious blend of familiarity and change. Faces that once roamed the college corridors were now adorned with the lines of time, yet the sparkle of recognition remained intact. Emma weaved her way through the crowd, nervously glancing around for familiar faces.

"Hey, Miss Beauty, here!"

The voice cut through the lively chatter, causing Emma to turn around. Her eyes lit up as she spotted Jennifer waving energetically. A wide smile painted Emma's face as she weaved through the crowd to join her friend.

"Jennifer! It's been ages!" Emma exclaimed, embracing her college friend in a tight hug.

The warmth of their friendship was palpable, and the years apart seemed to melt away. As Jennifer stepped back, she gestured to the others accompanying her.

"Emma, meet Stacy and Rebecca. Oh, and you remember Mark, right?"

Emma's eyes flickered to Mark, the lead vocalist of their college band. Despite the rumors swirling around about his mysterious marriage to a woman twice his age, there was an undeniable charm about him.

"Hey, Emma," Mark greeted with a casual smile, his voice carrying the magnetic aura that made him the heartthrob of their college days.

Suddenly, memories of late-night jam sessions and crowded gigs flooded Emma's mind.

"Hi, Mark. Long time no see," Emma replied, a hint of curiosity lingering in her eyes.

She could not help but wonder about the twists and turns in his life since they last crossed paths. As the group walked together, Jennifer could not contain her excitement.

"We were just reminiscing about the old times. Remember that crazy concert in our senior year?" she asked.

Laughter rippled through the group as they recalled the chaotic yet unforgettable moments of their college band's final performance. Mark went into the details of their fun-filled night, and for a moment, it felt like time had not moved at all.

"Remember, you threw the drink on my face?" Mark smirked; his eyes fixed on Emma.

A subtle blush adorned Emma's cheek, amplifying the playful atmosphere.

"Come on, it was an accident. You knew I tripped. And by the way, I did apologize, if you remember, Mr. Fussy," Emma retorted with a playful roll of her eyes.

Mark and the others burst into a fit of laughter. Enjoying the banter, Mark couldn't resist teasing Emma more.

"By the way, you never apologized. All you managed to say was,
'If you had watched your steps, I would not have spilled it on you,'" he mimicked Emma's words, sending the group into another round of laughter.

"Well, you still owe an apology to Mark then," Jennifer teased Emma, a mischievous wink directed at Mark.

"Why not if I spill another drink on him tonight?" Emma challenged, taking a glass of drink from the approaching server, her eyes sparkling with mischief.

The group erupted into laughter once again. Amid the cheerful chaos and lively banter, as Emma wiped tears from her eyes, she felt a gentle tap on her shoulder that pulled her from the reverie of reunion. The touch was so subtle it could have been mistaken for a trick of breeze. She turned around and found herself face to face with a figure from the past that time had tucked away in the recesses of her memory. His eyes met hers, a mix of surprise and joy reflecting in them.

"Emma!" he exclaimed, breaking into a wide smile.

"Liam! It's literally been ages," she replied, a grin spreading across her face as they embraced, the years between their last meeting melting away.

"Tell me about it," Liam replied, his eyes sparkling with the shared memories of late-night study sessions and laughter that echoed through the dorm halls.

"You haven't changed a bit," Emma exclaimed, taking in the details of his old fellow.

He still possessed a distinguished yet approachable charm. His black hair, meticulously styled, added an air of sophistication. His sharp, hazel eyes were still attractive. Clad in tailored suits, he also exuded a matchable elegance to Emma's.

"But you have. Look how beautiful you have grown since we last met!" Liam complimented her, making her go a deep shade of red.

"Oh, please! It's all the contouring," Emma waved her hand nonchalantly.

"You must be the first woman giving credit for your beauty to the makeup," said Liam.

"It is what it is, my friend," Emma shrugged.

Liam chuckled softly as he turned his attention to Jennifer and the group. After exchanging pleasantries with them, catching up on the years that had passed since graduation, Liam turned his attention to Emma once again.

"So, what's up with you?" asked Liam.

"Let's find a table first; my heels are killing me," said Emma, cursing her stilettos, which had grown uncomfortable with each passing minute.

They scanned the crowd and found an empty table.

"I'll be back in a minute," she informed Jennifer and Mark, who had been engrossed in some other discussion.

Jennifer acknowledged with a wave of the hand. In a quiet corner, away from the boisterous laughter and clinking glasses, Emma and Liam settled into empty chairs. The ambient hum of the party faded as they found their secluded spot.

Emma, eager for relief, kicked off her stilettos and rubbed her tired feet. "They are truly a nightmare. I am not gonna wear them again," she complained, her voice a mix of exasperation and relief.

Liam, amused, couldn't help but chuckle. "Why did you wear them in the first place?"

"Because they match," she replied matter-of-factly, a hint of a smile on her face. Liam grinned in response.

"Anyways, what have you been up to? How's the architecture world treating you?" Emma asked, genuinely curious.

A couple of years back, she learned about Liam running an architectural firm through an acquaintance. Liam ran a hand through his hair, a college habit that lingered.

He said, "Not complaining. Been quite busy with work, you know how it is. But, you know, success in my career isn't the only thing I've been searching for."

"Oh? And what might that be?" Emma said, arching an eyebrow.

"A deeper connection," he confessed, his gaze lingering on her.

The soft glow of ambient lights accentuated the sincerity in his eyes.

"What's the rush, Liam? Believe me, you'll find a perfect match soon," she told him.

"I just don't want all the good ones taken," Liam sighed deeply, his vulnerability met with Emma's laughter.

His grin mirrored her infectious amusement.

"Well, enough about me. What are you doing?" he asked her.

"I am a lead graphic designer at Pixel Weave Creations," Emma said as she motioned to the server to bring them more drinks.

"Wow, at Pixel Weave Creations! Impressive," Liam couldn't help but express his admiration. "Well, you must be making a lot of money then," he winked.

"Not as much as you, Mr. CEO," she retorted, making Liam laugh.

Their conversation flowed seamlessly, punctuated by bursts of laughter, and shared jokes that only old friends could appreciate. The atmosphere was filled with the electric energy of rekindled friendships.

As the night wore on, the DJ switched to a slow, soulful melody. Liam extended his hand, a playful glint in his eyes.

"Care for a dance?" he said.

"Why not?" Emma said excitedly, jumping to her feet at once.

Liam joined her, and they found themselves swaying to the rhythm, surrounded by the laughter of friends and the echoes of the past.

They kept swaying gracefully to the rhythm of a slow, melodic waltz. The music enveloped them like a gentle caress, and they both enjoyed the dance while they talked.

As their bodies moved in perfect harmony, their eyes locked in a magnetic gaze. It was as if time had slowed down, allowing them to relive a moment from the past that lingered in the corners of their memories. In that fleeting instant, the echoes of a shared secret whispered through the dance.

Liam, his strong hands guiding Emma with a tender touch, broke the silence.

"Emma," he murmured, a smile playing on his lips, "Do you remember that night under the starry sky?"

A subtle blush painted Emma's cheeks as she looked into Liam's hazel eyes, her voice soft as a breeze.

"Of course, Liam. How could I forget? You stole a kiss, and I couldn't decide whether to be outraged or flattered."

The music continued its enchanting melody, wrapping around them like a cocoon of reminiscent reverie. Liam chuckled, a hint of mischief in his eyes.

"The best decision I ever made," he said shamelessly with a smirk, "We were just so careless back then, stealing a kiss under the twinkling stars."

Emma's laughter danced in the air, a melody of its own.

"We were young and reckless, weren't we? But sorry to burst your bubble, you did not make a lasting impression," she said lightly.

"My bad!" he smiled.

A moment of shared understanding passed between them, with the weight of the past mingling with the present. Liam's gaze lingered on Emma; his expression filled with warmth.

"I cherish those memories, Emma, but we are different now," he told her.

Emma nodded, her eyes reflecting a mix of emotions.

"We have grown, and our friendship means everything to me," she responded.

They continued to dance, the steps weaving a silent dialogue between them. Liam's voice, like a gentle breeze, carried through the music.

"Let's not let that old memory jeopardize this moment and our friendship," he said.

Emma agreed, a smile tugging at the corners of her lips.

"Thank God; there is still a little sanity left in this world," she sighed as Liam broke into a wide grin.

As the dance concluded, they shared a gaze, understanding, and gratitude passing between them. The final notes of the music echoed in the air, sealing their vow to cherish their friendship, leaving the memories of that stolen kiss tucked away in the secret corners of their hearts.

Chapter 2: New Beginnings

As the evening swirled with laughter and the clinking of glasses, Emma and Liam joined their friends at a big round table in a corner of the hall. Munching on the food, the friends reminisced about their playful college days.

Just then, a young professor dressed in a lime green off-shoulder dress took the stage to deliver the concluding speech.

"Hey, everyone, I'm Professor Lydia – responsible for bidding you all farewell once again. I want to keep it short, so don't worry," she smiled.

"I'm so glad that you all showed up at this reunion. You might have left college behind, but the memories of your laughter and traces of mischievousness still linger through the building," Professor Lydia said, pointing at the graffiti on the ceiling of the hall.

The small crayon graffiti art had been on the ceiling for the last five years. The ceiling was so high that the staff found it difficult to clean. The only person who could remove it would have been the student who had broken into the hall at night after farewell and drawn it; only God knows how.

"I think it's time we uncover the talented face behind this mysterious masterpiece," Mark said, inviting a loud cheer from the former students.

"We can all gather again for it some other day," Professor Lydia said. "Tonight's already reached the climax."

"I am delighted to see you all doing amazing things in your lives, and I hope that you all continue to lead your best lives and achieve all of your dreams," she continued.

"I hope to see you all more often," she added before switching off the mic.

Mark leaned in towards Liam to whisper, "I cannot be the only one to think she was hot."

"Nope, you're certainly not," Liam confessed.

"How come I don't remember her?" Mark asked.

"She joined as an assistant professor just before we were about to graduate," Jennifer interrupted.

"I guess we can get to know her a little now," Mark said, getting up from his chair.

He ran a hand through his hair and fixed his shirt while walking up to Professor Lydia.

Liam looked at him and Lydia with keen interest. His eyes displayed affection for the professor – something Emma felt drawn towards.

"Are you sure you don't want to greet the 'Miss How-Come-I-Never-Noticed-Her-Before'?" she teased Liam.

Liam turned around to meet Emma's eyes. He sighed before slowly saying, "I don't chase; I attract."

"Huh! You wish," Emma mocked.

"You bet?" Liam asked, sitting straight up on his chair.

"On what? Is she coming up to you? To improve your chances of finding that spark with her," she said, giggling.

"Watch me! And learn," Liam replied, rolling his eyes.

He got up and made his way towards Mark, who was conversing with Professor Lydia and another student.

Liam pulled off his best move —charismatic confidence —and smoothly initiated a conversation with Mark, charming enough to draw Lydia's attention, who seemed intrigued by Liam's demeanor.

Sensing Lydia's growing interest, Mark attempted to introduce her to Liam. "Lydia, meet my friend Liam here. He's our resident architect extraordinaire," Mark introduced Liam.

"An architect? That's quite fascinating," Lydia said with a faint sparkle in her eyes.

"So, you must have a unique perspective on design and spaces," Lydia added. Her body was now completely turned towards Liam.

Liam nodded politely yet kept his responses concise — an art he had mastered to keep people interested in him.

"So, Liam, what inspired you to pursue architecture?" Lydia inquired, her eyes sparkling with curiosity.

"I've always been fascinated by how structures intertwine with human experiences. Architecture, to me, is about expressing stories through design," he responded with a warm smile.

Lydia smiled back, leaning in with interest.

"Stories through design, that's a beautiful perspective," she said. "I'm sure I didn't teach you that," she added with a hint of mischief in her voice.

"But you wish you did, don't you?" Liam joked, his eyes fixed on Lydia, a faint smile taking over his face.

Before Lydia could reply, Mark took his shot to regain inclusion in their conversation.

"No, Liam, Professor Lydia joined after we'd graduated," Mark interjected, but Lydia couldn't shake off Liam's effect on her.

"Yeah, but I could've joined earlier; not getting to know such brilliant students before is definitely a loss," she smirked.

Liam nodded, remaining quiet. Sensing his guarded demeanor, Lydia steered the conversation back to more casual topics.

"So, Liam, any interesting adventures from your college days?" she asked.

Every question of Lydia's that followed was met with Liam's calculated answers. Her lively energy contrasted with his quiet thoughtfulness. Despite her attempts to engage him more, he remained reserved.

Soon, Liam excused himself from the conversation, citing the need to check on something. As he walked away, Lydia's eyes bore into his back, tracing his footsteps. It was a sight that made it apparent to Emma that she'd lost the bet.

As her eyes moved to the winning side, she sensed a mismatch of energies. A flicker of empathy crawled onto her bones. She knew how badly Liam sought the kind of connection that remained elusive to him.

"Tough crowd, huh?" she joked as he approached her.

"Sometimes, energies just don't align, no matter how much you want them to," Liam said, sighing softly.

Emma nodded in understanding, offering a reassuring smile.

"Well, there are plenty of stars in the sky, Liam. Sometimes, the one you seek might not be the right constellation for you," she said.

Liam nodded and regained his composure, attempting not to seem too emotional.

"FYI, I won the bet," he said almost smugly.

"So you actually meant it?" she scoffed.

Their eyes met, holding a silent promise of more shared moments to come. Emma shifted in her seat, then leaned in to say, "Okay, CEO heartthrob, what do you want?"

"What about a rematch in beer pong? You owe me that anyway," Liam suggested.

Emma chuckled, the memories flooding back.

"You wish, Liam. I seem to recall wiping the floor with you back in the day," she replied.

"Details, details," Liam quipped, taking a playful sip of his drink.

***

As the night wore on, the reunion reached its conclusion, and the crowd of students started leaving the hall. Amidst the shared laughter of the old friends, Emma walked out of the college corridors. Leaving the echoes of their banter cascading through the walls once again.

Upon reaching the outside of the building, a surprise caught them unguarded. It had started raining. It reminded them how San Francisco's weather can change suddenly, with fog and light rain coming unexpectedly.

"No way!" exclaimed Mark while throwing his hands in the air.

"Damn it, I can't find a ride in this weather," said Emma while scrolling through a cab-booking app.

"You didn't drive here?" Jennifer asked, surprised.

Before Emma could reply, Liam quickly interrupted as if he had been waiting for the moment.

"I can drop you," he offered, shrugging. "Going in the same direction anyway…"

"No, you don't know where I live," Emma said with disbelief.

"Being mysterious might have been your goal. But Ms. Emma, you gave away too much," Liam said, leaning in and winking at Emma.

"Whatever!" Emma rolled her eyes before turning to Jennifer, who was busy tapping the cell phone screen.

"Hey Jennifer, could you drive me home?" Emma asked.

"I would love to, but my boyfriend is coming to pick me up. We've got some plans," Jennifer said with a mix of concern and an apologetic tone.

Liam chuckled, drawing Emma's attention back towards him. Emma stared at him blankly for a moment.

"I hope your driving isn't as bad as your manners," Emma said while walking towards the parking lot.

Liam followed her, putting off his coat.

"You might take this as well," Liam said while offering his coat to Emma, who was shivering in her off-shoulder dress.

"How masterful you are!" she grinned, taking Liam's coat.

"You could have simply thanked me," Liam replied, stopping abruptly beside a shiny black Mercedes.

He leaned against his car with a sly grin on his face. As Emma approached, adjusting her coat, she took a look at the car and said with a playful smirk, "So, Mr. Architect extraordinaire, is this your grand chariot?"

"Ah, you mock my trusted steed," Liam teased, opening the car door for Emma. "But fear not, fair maiden, for this steed shall safely transport you to your abode."

Emma chuckled, sliding into the passenger seat.

"I hope this noble steed knows the way, or else I might end up in a medieval castle instead of my apartment," she said.

"With my flawless navigation skills, you're in no danger of ending up in a different century," Liam quipped, starting the engine.

As they drove through the streets bathed in raindrops and the soft glow of city lights, a comfortable silence settled between them. The memories of their college days lingered, wrapping around them like a comforting blanket.

"So, Emma," Liam broke the silence, his tone softer now, "do you ever think about that night?"

Emma pretended not to catch up.

"What night?" she said, her eyes fixed on the road.

"Seriously? You can do better, Ms. Aspiring Actor," Liam said, apparently annoyed.

Emma glanced at him, and a chuckle broke out.

"Oh, that night!" she exclaimed.

As she continued to recall, a mix of excitement and hesitation settled in her eyes.

"Sometimes. It's one of those memories that refuses to fade, you know?" she added.

"Yeah," Liam murmured, his gaze fixed on the road ahead. "It feels like it's always there, just beneath the surface."

Their shared glance held many unspoken emotions, a silent understanding passing between them amidst the faint hum of raindrops hitting the car's surface.

"But you know," Emma said, breaking the moment with a mischievous glint, "I still maintain it was you who stole that kiss, not the other way around."

Liam chuckled, a warmth creeping into his voice.

"Is that your version of rewriting history, Emma?" he asked her.

"Absolutely," she replied, her laughter echoing in the car. "And I'm sticking to it."

"So what happened between you and Lydia tonight?" she asked, bringing them back to the present.

"Well, Lydia's nice. She's successful and smart, clearly interested in me, but..." Liam trailed off, searching for the right words.

"But what?" Emma interrupted. "Don't tell me that you didn't feel the spark and all."

"Why not? It's important for me," Liam argued, slowing down the car; his attention was wholly diverted to Emma.

"You need to spend time with someone to find the connection. Go on a few dates with her. Who knows, you may grow to like each other," Emma explained.

"The connection is felt, not created! If I hadn't felt the spark with her in the first meeting, I would have had no interest in the second meeting whatsoever," Liam replied.

"So what do you plan on doing, Mr. CEO? Staying single forever?" Emma asked.

"Don't worry, I'm too handsome and successful for that," Liam smirked, inviting a chuckle from Emma.

"You're also too full of yourself," Emma teased before giving Liam directions to her apartment. "You can stop right after taking a left turn from here."

As they pulled up to Emma's apartment building, they lingered in the car's silence.

"Thanks for the ride, Liam," Emma said softly, breaking the ice.

Liam turned to her, a gentle smile gracing his lips.

"Anytime, Emma. Maybe next time, I'll make sure the steed takes us on a proper adventure," he replied.

Emma burst into laughter, suddenly stopped, and shifted in her seat. "You know what? I've got an idea," she excitedly said to Liam.

Liam appeared intrigued, raising his eyebrows.

"What now?" he asked.

"I know the key to unlock our connection quest," Emma replied, her eyes gleaming excitedly.

"Right, ma'am, enlighten me then," Liam said, turning towards Emma.

"There's no way I am giving you this idea just like that," Emma teased while opening the car door.

"What?" Liam protested.

"Let's have a beer pong rematch next weekend?" she said, stepping out of the car.

She paused for a moment, leaning back through the open window.

"Thanks again, Liam. And hey, keep practicing that dance. I might challenge you to dance someday," she told him.

 Liam laughed, a warm twinkle in his eyes.

"Looking forward to it, Emma. Have a good night," he said.

As Emma hurriedly made her way to her apartment, dodging the raindrops, Liam remained seated in his car for a moment longer. His eyes traced the emptiness of the street with a contemplative expression.

The drizzle outside seemed to echo the complexity of his thoughts. Starting the engine, Liam pulled out of the parking lot and made his way through the damp streets. He was already counting down the days until the next weekend.

Chapter 3: Pacts and Playful Promises

A message beep made Emma open her eyes with a deep sigh and underlying hints of frustration. Saturday mornings meant nothing but some quality meditation for her – a time with no disturbances appreciated.

Sitting cross-legged on a yoga mat, Emma lifted her hands from her knees to pick up her phone. With the thought that it could be Mark who was interrupting her favorite part of the day, Emma started boiling with anger.

Mark had been hitting up her all week, pestering her to design posters for his underground jukebox sessions, or maybe it was a standup comedy gig. Emma didn't pay attention whenever he called. She was either busy meeting with a client or in the middle of a very important project.

"For God's sake! It's 7 a.m. Ma-" Emma suddenly stopped as she read "Mr. CEO" on the screen. It was a message from Liam, the one she'd been waiting for the whole week.

Why? Emma didn't know, but getting to know him again after a long time was like a new game design project.

Emma had started her career as a graphic designer for games development, something she had a great interest in. Still, for the past several months, she'd only been getting publication design projects. It wasn't bad – she loved her job, but the adrenaline rush that designing games brought her was incomparable.

"You up?" Liam's message read.

A faint smile appeared on Emma's face. Her glaring eyes softened, and furrowed brows straightened.

Emma eased off her yoga pose and started tapping on the screen as she thought of a perfect reply – not so rude or cheesy! Perhaps it was way too early in the day to strike the right balance between the two.

Before she could think of anything, her phone started buzzing. Mr. CEO was calling!

Emma was surprised, but she was also panicking.

"Hello?" she answered, getting up on her feet.

"Oh Hi! So, Pixel Weave keeps you up even on an early Saturday morning. I thought you wouldn't answer – snoring in your deep sleep, you know," Liam said.

His voice sounded as sophisticated as he appeared – attractive and elegant. "If that's what you thought, why are you taking your chances?" Emma replied.

She was trying to sound the opposite of what she was feeling – sheer excitement. She walked around her balcony, her steps as light as a bird's feather. Her eyes traced the timeline of San Francisco's tall towers, standing proud against the sky.

"I am very particular about my work-life balance. FYI, I was doing yoga – in my precious meditation time - and a certain somebody disturbed me," added Emma.

"Wow, that's great! I called yo-" Liam said something, but the rest of his words were carried away by what sounded like heavy winds.

Emma told Liam that she couldn't hear him clearly, and Liam quickly made a few adjustments and asked her again after a moment. "Yes, your voice is much clearer now," Emma replied, folding her yoga mat.

Her morning was already off to a good start.

Liam's deep voice, soothing accent, and captivating conversational skills had already released a good amount of happy hormones for Emma. Her otherwise quiet apartment echoed with his giggles.

"Excuse the disturbance. I come to the beach for a morning run, and the wind here is quite strong," explained Liam.

"By the way, I called you to remind you that it's the weekend! I hope you haven't forgotten our childish beer-pong rematch," he added.

"Yes, of course, I remember," Emma replied.

She remembered what they agreed on, but she didn't know that Liam would actually make time out of his busy schedule.

He offered to pick Emma up from her place at 7 p.m., and Emma agreed. She hung up the phone call and quickly dialed a colleague's number. She had made movie plans with her two workmates or, to be precise, another publication design project—something Emma would never prefer over a game development gig.

She kept calling, but none of her colleagues answered. Her gaze fell on the wall clock; it wasn't even 8 a.m. Emma quickly ended the call, typed a message, and sent it to their group instead. It read:

"Girls, something urgent came up! Can't hang out tonight!"

***

"Already 7:15? So, I guess Mr. CEO isn't that punctual!" Emma muttered.

She checked the time on a vintage Rolex strapped on her slim wrist with brown leather.

Suddenly, Emma's phone buzzed. It was Liam calling!

"Hello?" Emma answered, managing to sound less gloomy.

"Yeah, I'm downstairs," Liam said, sounding excited for the evening.

"I'm coming," Emma replied hurriedly, hanging up the phone.

Emma had picked a perfect outfit for the evening – a perfect mix of trendy yet cozy. She carried her lilac cross-body bag, matching with her lilac crop top. She had paired the top with black bell bottoms and delicately tied her auburn locks into a high ponytail.

She climbed downstairs and walked towards Liam's car, fixing a few strands that playfully fell on her forehead. She looked comfortably gorgeous, making Liam's jaw drop. However, he wanted to appear calm and not make it obvious that he'd given in to Emma's effortless beauty.

"You look pretty," Liam said as soon as she hopped in the passenger seat.

Emma turned around to Liam and quickly analyzed Liam's outfit from head to toe. She was impressed with Liam's perfect blend of casual yet classy attire. He looked handsome in a white tee under a sleek black leather jacket, which he had paired with black jeans.

"You don't look too bad either!" she remarked, putting on her seat belt.

"So where are we going?" she asked.

"Oh, I didn't think much about it. Let's go to the restaurant I usually go to," Liam replied, trying to conceal the four hours he spent selecting the perfect dinner spot.

Suddenly, he felt the need to appear unbothered in front of Emma – as if the evening wasn't much of a big deal for him. While, in fact, it was.

When he dropped Emma off at her place after the reunion, Liam might have considered all the possibilities of their bond, but he had surely underestimated Emma's charm. In the middle of the meetings, important phone calls, and every car ride throughout the week, thoughts of Emma lingered in Liam's head. He didn't know reuniting with her after all this time would interest him this much.

"Sure!" Emma replied, reclaiming Liam's attention, which was fixed on analyzing his own strange emotions.

"Huh?" asked Liam, confused.

"The restaurant… sure, let's go! I'm starving," Emma said, flashing a bright smile that lit up Liam's car's otherwise dark interior.

"Yeah, of course," Liam quipped, clearing his throat.

They hadn't gone farther than a mile when it started drizzling. The raindrops fell on the windshield, blurring the vision. Liam turned on the wiper, clearing his view of the street.

"Can this fair maiden still trust your flawless navigation skills, or is landing in a medieval castle still a possibility?" Emma asked, grinning.

"Do you have a habit of literally memorizing every word of each conversation you have?" asked Liam.

Emma's cheeks turned red. No, she hadn't been replaying her reunion with Liam in her head. At least that's what she wanted to portray because why would she spend this much thought on reuniting with a college friend?

"I happen to have a good memory, especially when it comes to terrorizing experiences, and your driving does qualify for my criteria of a terrorizing experience!" she exclaimed, rolling her eyes.

"I drive just perfectly. Yes, I go faster than others on the road – but that's just a habit of mine. You know, being ahead of the rest!" Liam said, winking and speeding up a little.

"By the way, I hope you're not cold because I'm not going to offer you my jacket tonight," Liam added, teasing her again.

"Don't worry because the drizzling will soon stop. I read the weather forecast today," she smirked.

Amidst their playful banter, the drive ended as Liam pulled over in front of an exquisite dining place. It had stopped drizzling as the forecast noted, but Emma was still troubled.

She looked at the grand entrance of the restaurant and then the queue of luxurious cars parked outside it. She held her gasp, not letting it leave her mouth and turned to look at Liam. Such a place wasn't to her taste. She loved being somewhere modest and among people she could be comfortable with.

"Liam, can we please go somewhere else?" Emma asked, taking a deep breath as if she were trying to hide her disappointment.

"Why? This place has-" Liam started mumbling.

"This place is too elegant. I want to go somewhere more lively and fun. I know a better place. Let's go there," Emma interrupted.

"Okay!" Liam agreed, although he was downright disappointed.

He pulled out of the restaurant's parking lot and, following Emma's instructions, ended up at Valencia Street – a vibrant street with a string of restaurants, bars, and cafes on each side. Getting a parking slot there was difficult on a weekend, but they somehow managed.

Emma got out of the car and started walking through a crowd of people, with Liam closely following her. They both entered a super busy dining place full of tourists. Liam looked around the place; this restaurant had a much humbler interior than the one he'd made a reservation in. However, it wasn't bad.

"This place is chaotic!" Liam exclaimed, sitting down on a wooden chair across from Emma.

"It's lively!" Emma said while waving at the waiter.

She refused to take the menu and ordered the restaurant's special sushi platters - something she would never get tired of eating. Liam decided to go with Emma's recommendation.

A few minutes later, a waiter arrived with two giant platters of various sushi and tempting condiments. Munching on the finger-licking good meal, Liam asked the question he'd been waiting to ask her the whole week.

"So Emma, you're pretty, educated, and doing quite well professionally. How come you are still single?" he asked, leaning over the table.

"I hate to admit it, but I'm not good at social interactions, flirting and all," Emma replied before asking, "What about you? Why are you not seeing anyone?"

"I've been on a couple of dates, but it's not easy to manage with my busy schedule, and also, I couldn't feel the 'connection' with anyone," Liam told Emma.

"If that's the case, I have a solution: a world where you're not yet – dating apps," Emma said cheerfully.

"Oh no, no. Thank you very much, but no," Liam said.

"C'mon, you can meet so many people there based on your interests and hobbies. It's like a perfect and the most practical way of finding the spark you're looking for," Emma explained.

"It's not that simple," Liam replied hesitantly.

"It's so simple, Liam. You write down your interests and hobbies, and this app will match your profile with people of similar interests. You talk to them and even go on a couple of dates if you like each other," Emma explained enthusiastically, sitting on the edge of her seat.

"And you think I haven't considered this method?" Liam asked, sitting back with his hands crossed against his chest. "I don't know how to make a good profile."

"Exactly why we need to make a deal, Mr. CEO," said Emma, cleaning off her mouth with a napkin.

"Now, what's that?" asked Liam, bending over the table.

"I know how to make a good profile. I can help you with that, but in return, you need to help me with something, too," Emma said.

"Go on, I'm listening," Liam said, his hazel eyes looking straight into Emma's dark, expressive eyes.

Emma was already impressed with Liam's sense of humor, and he was also quite good at flirting. It was something she had noticed when he had a brief but impactful interaction with Professor Lydia.

"Teach me the art of flirting and making the first move without embarrassing myself or looking awkward. In return, I'll help you set up a profile on the dating app," Emma offered.

"So, there is actually something that you need my help with," teased Liam.

"Nothing's free in this world, you know. I'm going to help you with something; you need to do this much in return," Emma explained.

"Okay, deal!" Liam agreed, extending a hand to shake.

"Deal," Emma said, taking his hand.

They wrapped up the dinner, but it was too early for them to part ways just yet; they still needed to do their part of the deal. Following Emma's recommendation, the duo went to one of the busiest bars on the street.

"Don't tell me you're a regular even here," Liam said to Emma, his eyes tracing the rowdy group of customers screaming at the top of their lungs.

"Just a few times," Emma replied.

They both settled on a table in one corner of a dimly lit bar and rolled out the promised game of beer pong. Amidst laughter and a crazy game of beer pong, Emma said something to Liam, but her words were drowned by loud music mixed with deafening chants and the clinking of glasses.

"Give me your phone so I can create your profile," Emma repeated more loudly.

Liam handed his phone to Emma, and she got busy tapping on the screen.

She asked Liam if he had a favorite picture of himself. When he couldn't decide, they both started scrolling through his photo gallery to select Liam's best pictures.

"Since we've added the pictures, all we need to do is come up with the best bio," she said.

Liam, having no expertise in that sphere, returned to the game. As he missed his shots, he continued chugging in the glasses of beer.

"Done! Your profile is ready, by the way," Emma chirped, returning Liam's phone to him.

"Now, it's your turn to do your part of the deal," she added.

"Right! I'm a little tipsy, so don't mind me," Liam said.

He stumbled while going over to Emma's side of the table. Then, he took her hand and dragged her to the bar.

"So, do you see the guy in a blue tee? Go to him and say what I tell you," Liam said, giving Emma instructions.

"What? No, no, that's too direct. Also, I don't like that blue tee!" Emma said, shaking her head.

"What about the guy in white and blue stripes on the dance floor?" Liam asked, pointing at another man.

"Well, he's nice, but he's on the dance floor! How am I supposed to break through all that noise?" asked Emma.

"Here, let me show you," said Liam, grabbing Emma by her waist tightly.

His eyes met Emma's dark gaze, and his hold turned delicate.

The bar's dim lights cast a warm hue over Emma's eyes, making her look straight out of a fairytale. The loud music started fading away while the loud chants of people submerged into the hushed whispers of their hearts.

Emma, usually guarded, felt the fortress around her crumble to the ground while Liam's fingers traced an invisible pattern on Emma's back. He leaned in, cupping Emma's face with his other hand, and slowly pushed her head closer to his – closer enough so that his lips traced Emma's soft and plump ones.

He drew back to see Emma's reaction. She had closed her eyes in approval, her hands holding him by his neck. Then, she pulled him closer to her, and suddenly, the whole world fell quiet. As they kissed, Emma and Liam could only hear the rhythm of each other's hearts.

In that intimate moment, they let go of all the reservations in their hearts and let their unplanned romance take root not in grand gestures but in reveling in the embrace, finding a soothing sensation in each other's arms.

Chapter 4: Unexpected Chemistry

The next morning, Emma sat straight on her bed, staring blankly at the mirror across her bed, overwhelmed by the unexpected encounter with Liam. Her mind recalled every tiny detail of her passionate kiss with Liam last night.

While taking a hot shower, brewing a cup of coffee, or looking out of the car window, Emma's hand would unknowingly reach up to her lips, reminiscing about the unforgettable events of last night and the feeling of Liam's lips on hers. But she'd come back to her senses just as quickly, trying to shrug the thoughts off her head.

"I should not be thinking about this at work," she muttered to herself while entering her office.

"I hope you had a terrible weekend after ditching us at the last moment," her colleague rolled her eyes while waving at Emma.

"Good morning, Hannah! I'm so sorry for calling it off at the last minute. Something urgent came up," Emma replied, sitting in her seat.

Hannah was quick to notice the dark circles around Emma's eyes, revealing how tired she'd been. She leaned closer to Emma before asking her in a hushed voice, "Hey, everything good?"

"Yes. Why do you ask?" asked Emma, puzzled.

"You look a little tired. What happened??" Hannah questioned, worry evident on her face. Emma got deep into her head as she weighed in on her complicated feelings: a mix of weird excitement, swirling guilt, and a looming sadness.

"Nothing!" Emma interrupted the train of her thoughts. "I just put in too much effort to help a friend of mine. Perhaps a little too much effort?"

"What help? Wait, who is this friend? You barely do anything except work!" Hannah rebutted.

"Oh, I recently reconnected with my college friend after a while, like at the reunion I told you about. Yeah... so he..." Emma tried her best to search for the right words, but her heart started beating so fast that she lost her composure. "That's weird," she mumbled to herself, taking deep breaths to stop herself from going into full panic mode as Hannah looked at her with concern.

"The meeting room in 5, everyone!"

Emma breathed a sigh of relief as she was saved by the dramatic entry of her manager, who called everyone in for a weekly meeting—a regular Monday ritual! She was sure Hannah would grill her for details later, but for now, she could delay explaining her messed-up situation until she could make better sense of it.

She got up from her seat, picked up her laptop, and went on to attend the meeting, with Hannah hesitantly following behind. Indulging herself with excessive work, Emma spent the whole week trying to forget the weekend until it was, once again, knocking on the door.

Not breaking her Saturday morning routine amidst the ongoing crisis in her life, Emma did yoga, which only made her angrier instead of relaxed. Despite her many attempts, she hadn't stopped looking at her cell phone the whole week in hopes that Liam would call. Every time she felt her phone buzz, she would check it immediately, but it was never the one she was waiting to hear from.

Now that it was Saturday—a whole week since the incident—Emma was only disappointed. She had also considered calling him to ask whether he'd been keeping up with the dating app or needed her help, but she couldn't find enough courage.

"What's the best way to beat embarrassment?" She typed on Google but put away her phone without even checking the answers.

After having breakfast, she did laundry, cleaned, and completed all the chores, only to later find herself sitting idly in front of the LED screen in her lounge. This was not how she'd been planning to spend her weekend. She looked outside the window and noticed the yellow sky turning blue as the sun was about to set.

Emma left a message in her friends' group, asking if they were down for a 'club night,' but found no luck. She loosely fell back on the couch, staring at the ceiling. This week had been too tiring and taxing on her brain; Emma needed a rejuvenating break.

"I can go by myself," she said, getting up from the couch. She put on her favorite blue jumpsuit that was stylish and warm for the evening, checked her phone once again just in case, and murmured "whatever" to herself before leaving for the night out.

The sun dipped low on the horizon, casting a warm glow across the city streets. At the crossroads, just outside the club, Emma got out of the cab and, to her surprise, found herself face-to-face with Liam.

They both stood still, motionless, since it was their first interaction after the unexpected kiss at the club.

"Hey, what a surprise?" Liam managed to conceal his awkwardness.

"I didn't think I'd run into you here," said Emma, managing an awkward smile.

"You've got company?" asked Liam as they both entered the club. "I'm here with my friends."

"No, I just came here by myself... I'm a regular here, remember?" she chuckled.

"Of course, I remember. You can join us if you want; I'll introduce you to my workmates, and I'm also me-" Liam's words were interrupted by a loud cheer from his group of friends.

"You are late again!" complained one of Liam's friends.

"Had a meeting, sorry!" replied Liam before gesturing at Emma. "By the way, meet my college friend, Emma."

"Hello, there." Multiple voices rang in her eyes. A warm welcome brought a soft smile to Emma's face, taking away her hesitation.

"I hope you guys don't mind if I join you all," Emma asked.

"Oh no, not at all!" they replied. "We're glad to be in the company of such a pretty woman," one of them added.

The quaint club pulsated with life as Emma and Liam sat among their friends, exchanging stories and laughter. Emma explained to them the nature of her work and day-to-day tasks while they briefed her on their line of work.

Amidst the chatter and clinks of glasses, an unspoken tension lingered between Emma and Liam, who sat beside each other. Their eyes met now and then, making Liam sense the need for an explanation, but he couldn't muster up the courage.

As the evening progressed, an unplanned incident unfolded, drawing Emma and Liam into a world of their own. Their hands brushed accidentally under the table, sending a spark of electricity through them. Instead of immediately pulling back, Liam and Emma held each other's hands more firmly, fingers intertwining in an almost instinctive gesture.

They exchanged a quick glance, both aware of the quiet connection that had formed between them. Surrounded by the exciting club air and the laughter of their friends, their intertwined hands became a silent acknowledgment of something they dared not speak about.

Emma felt warmth from their joined hands and assumed that Liam would feel the same. Liam's gaze met Emma's, and he sighed deeply. He cleared his throat and leaned over to say something.

Emma mirrored Liam, offering him her attention and anticipating the words he was about to say—the elephant in the room.

Their conversation began with a shared awkwardness, the air heavy with unspoken questions. Yet, as they delved into their feelings and the night's events at the club, a sense of honesty enveloped them.

Liam spoke in a soft tone, "Emma, that kiss..." He paused for a moment, reading Emma's eyes. By this time, she'd already mastered the art of concealing her feelings.

"It was just a spur-of-the-moment thing," he began. "Please! I've been thinking about it, about us, and I don't want that night to affect this rekindled bond of friendship."

Emma nodded, her eyes meeting his. "Me too. It was unexpected, and I understand, of course," she said.

"Are we good?" Liam asked again for reassurance, receiving a soft smile from Emma.

This wasn't the kind reaction Emma had hoped for, but she knew it was right. She appreciated it honestly, believing it would strengthen their mutual understanding. She took a deep breath and decided to switch back to her witty self.

"So? How's meeting with new people coming along?" asked Emma.

Liam hesitated before replying.

"It's been okay, I guess. There is nothing too serious except that I am meeting with someone tonight," he said.

"That's cool! I told you that my suggestion would work. I hope it goes well," Emma said, sipping a huge glass of beer.

"I'm curious about this person... When is she coming?" she asked amusingly, looking around.

"That's her," Liam said, pointing towards a blonde girl trying to enter the club.

She looked stunning in a body-hugging, dark brown, over-lapped short dress, and the woman waved at Liam, who was already on his way to welcome his date.

Liam and the woman took a table at the other corner of the club. They shook hands and quickly ordered a few drinks. A few minutes passed by, and a couple of beats immersed the club into a new, more intimate energy. Emma noticed herself staring at Liam and his date.

Feeling conscious again, she tore her attention away from the couple and realized that Liam's friends were already grooving on the dance floor, and she was left all by herself. She chugged another glass of beer when a strange voice claimed her attention.

"Hey, you don't seem to have company," interrupted a fair, almost pale white guy. His unfathomable, golden-brown eyes contrasted exceptionally with his light-toned face.

"Do you mind if I join you?" he politely asked, and Emma nodded. She was impressed with his striking features and a little too lonely to refuse him.

"I'm Alex," he said.

"Emma!" replied Emma. "Do you come to this club often?"

"Not really, but I might start if it means running into someone as charming as you," Alex replied, bringing a bright smile to Emma's face.

"Smooth talker, aren't you?" Emma remarked, staring straight into Alex's eyes.

"Only when I'm talking to someone who catches my eye," Alex grinned.

Practicing Liam's techniques, Emma teased Alex, "Oh, I see. So, you're saying I caught your eye?"

"Absolutely. From the moment I saw you, actually," Alex replied, offering her to join him on the dance floor. Without a second thought, she took Alex's hand and followed him.

"Well, I hope I don't scare you off with my amazing dance moves," Emma playfully quipped.

"Let's just say your dance moves are a bonus to your overall awesomeness," Alex grinned, impressed by Emma's subtle dance moves.

"Flattery will get you everywhere, won't it?" Emma asked.

"It only matters if it gets me another dance with you. What do you say?" Alex didn't miss the chance.

"Hmm, I might consider it if you promise not to step on my toes," Emma teased.

"Deal! I'll make sure to keep my feet in check," Alex replied.

An exchange of witty remarks and shared stories about the club filled the air. The conversation with Alex was interesting but insufficient to keep Emma's attention from diverting to Liam.

In the dimly lit ambiance, Liam's gaze, too, found its way to Emma more often than he'd like to admit, his eyes expressing a depth of interest for which he didn't have any explanation. Emma, catching his intense stare, felt her cheeks flush with a mix of excitement and nervousness.

As the night went on, Emma and Liam both felt a mix of jealousy and confusion. Even though they were with other people, they couldn't stop thinking about each other. They exchanged quick looks and tried to act normal, but inside, they were struggling with their growing feelings. The night ended with many unsaid things between them, leaving Emma and Liam feeling a bit lost as they tried to figure out what it all meant.

Chapter 5: Tensions and Confessions

The chaotic atmosphere of the club faded into the past, replaced by the professional ambiance of Liam's architectural firm. It had been some time since their unexpected double date at the club, and both Liam and Emma had managed to put the awkwardness behind them.

Amid a lingering discomfort, Liam and Emma decided to pause their pursuit of new dates. The weight of hidden emotions steered them away from the bond they shared. Both sought refuge from the internal turmoil and buried themselves in their work.

They tried to get busy in the hum of the office, lined up projects and long meetings, hoping to drown out the echoes of that fateful night at the club. The buzz of productivity served as a temporary escape, a shield against the emotional chaos that simmered beneath the surface until one day, fate brought them closer to each other once again.

One day, Liam was discussing potential collaborators for an upcoming project with his colleague Sarah. "Liam, Emma's company could be a great fit for this project. They have the creative edge we need, and Emma herself is a talented designer," she said.

Liam's eyes lit up at the suggestion.

"You know, Sarah, that's a brilliant idea. Emma does have the skills and vision we're looking for. Plus, we've worked together before, and I believe we can make a great team."

With Sarah's recommendation in mind, Liam and his team arranged a series of meetings and discussions with Emma's company. The more they delved into the possibilities, the more it became evident that their collaboration could lead to something exceptional.

Finally, Liam made the crucial phone call to Emma to convince her.

"Emma, I'm not saying this because we are friends. I truly believe in our potential as a team. Your company is the perfect fit for our project, and I'd be honored if you'd join us. What do you say?" he said in a hopeful tone.

Emma hesitated for a moment, remembering their club rendezvous and the undeniable chemistry they shared.

"Liam, I appreciate your confidence in us. Let's put the past behind us and focus on this project. I'm in," she replied after a thoughtful pause.

With both of them committed to the professional endeavor ahead, Liam's architectural firm and Emma's design company started a new chapter, ready to create something extraordinary together.

***

On the day of the first work meeting, Emma arrived at Liam's architectural firm dressed in smart business attire, ready to discuss the project. As she entered the sleek and modern office space, she couldn't help but feel a reminiscence of their kiss at the club.

Looking equally professional in a suit and tie, Liam greeted Emma with a polite smile. "Emma, it's good to see you again," he said, his tone friendly but with a hint of lingering tension.

Emma returned the smile, determined to keep things strictly professional. "Likewise, Liam. Let's focus on the project and get the job done," she replied.

As they began to work together on the project, their initial awkwardness gradually gave way to a shared sense of purpose and collaboration. They discussed ideas, exchanged feedback, and spent long hours working side by side, getting to know each other in a new domain.

One afternoon, while they were reviewing design concepts, Liam couldn't help but smile as he said, "Emma, your creative vision is truly remarkable. I'm glad we're working together on this."

Emma smiled back at him, appreciating the compliment.

"Thank you, Liam. Your insights on the architectural aspects are invaluable. I believe our combined strengths will make this project exceptional."

They continued to exchange ideas, offering constructive feedback to each other. It wasn't long before their discussions turned into animated debates, each pushing the other to think outside the box. It was during one of these debates that Liam realized how much he enjoyed the dynamic between them.

"You know, Emma," he said, leaning back in his chair, "I've missed our intellectual debates. It's refreshing to have someone challenge my ideas."

Emma chuckled, her eyes sparkling with enthusiasm.

"Likewise, Liam. It's been a while since I've had a collaborator who pushes me to explore new creative avenues," she said.

As the days turned into weeks, they spent long hours working side by side, fine-tuning their project to perfection. Late one evening, as they were finalizing the design, Emma looked at Liam.

"I have to admit, I wasn't sure how this would go when we first started, but I'm glad we took this chance," she said.

Liam nodded, his gaze locked with hers. "Me too, Emma. This project has not only been professionally rewarding but also a reminder of how well we work together."

Over time, their professional connection sparked an even stronger chemistry. As they worked together to bring their creative vision to life, the attraction that they concealed only intensified.

***

The soft glow of the office lights spilled into Emma's small cubicle as she worked on her computer. The rhythmic tapping of keys filled the air while she focused on her tasks. Her phone buzzed; it was her colleague, Hannah.

"Hey, stranger. How do you like your new office?" Hannah asked.

Emma grinned and pulled up a chair, settling in with an air of curiosity.

"What's up, Emma? Spill the beans," said Hannah.

Emma hesitated for a moment, then took a deep breath.

"You know, Hannah, there's something I need to tell you," she said.

Hannah's voice grew stern.

"Go on," she said.

"It's about Liam," Emma admitted, her cheeks tinged with a hint of pink.

"Liam? The one from the college reunion, or maybe I should say the kiss at the club?" Hannah teased.

Emma nodded.

"Yeah, that Liam. It's strange, but working closely with him on this project has made me see him in a different light."

Hannah sensed there was more to the story.

"Different, how?" she asked.

Emma smiled, her eyes sparkling with enthusiasm.

"Hannah, I've been so impressed by him. He's not just a great professional partner, but I've realized I really like him. I can't stop thinking about him."

Hannah grinned, clearly delighted by Emma's revelation.

"Well, well, Miss Emma, it sounds like you've got a little crush on Liam."

Emma rolled her eyes playfully.

"I know, I know. But it's not that simple. We share a strong bond, and I don't want to mess things up. Plus, I have no idea how he feels about me," she said.

"You've got to be honest with him, Emma. Life's too short to keep your feelings hidden. And who knows, maybe he's feeling the same way," Hannah mused.

Emma nodded, a mixture of excitement and nervousness in her expression. "You're right, Hannah. I need to talk to him and see where this goes."

"That's the spirit! Just be yourself, and everything will fall into place. And if it doesn't, at least you'll know you gave it a shot," Hannah said.

As Emma continued to work in her cubicle, her thoughts were consumed by the newfound feelings she had for Liam. She couldn't ignore the growing connection between them, and with Hannah's support, she felt ready to take the next step and be open with him about her emotions.

***

One evening, Liam found himself at a local bar with his work partner, Sarah. The dimly lit atmosphere and the low hum of chatter provided temporary relief from the workload.

As they sat at the bar, clinking glasses after a successful presentation, Sarah noticed Liam's distracted demeanor.

With concern etched on her face, she leaned in and asked, "Hey, Liam, everything all right?"

Liam sighed, taking a sip of his drink before responding.

"Not really. Things have been complicated lately," he admitted.

Sarah observed him closely, sensing that there was more to his troubles than he was letting on. "Let me guess... is it about Emma?" she asked, her tone gentle.

Liam appeared surprised by her question.

"Wait, how do you know about her?"

"Well, all of our friends know about it, thanks to your chemistry at the club," she said, sipping on her drink. "But it seems like there's more to the story. You've been acting differently lately, Liam."

Liam hesitated for a moment, then decided to open up.

"You're right, Sarah. It's not just about that. I've been feeling... conflicted about Emma."

Sarah nodded, encouraging him to share his true feelings.

"Tell me more. What's really going on?" she said.

Liam recounted the intimate moments with Emma.

"I don't know what it is, Sarah, but being around Emma just feels right," he confessed, his professional facade slipping.

Sarah studied Liam for a moment, a knowing look in her eyes.

"Liam, it sounds like you're hiding your true feelings behind professionalism. Maybe it's time to be open with Emma about how you really feel."

Liam sighed, realizing that Sarah was right. He had been trying to suppress his emotions, but it was becoming increasingly difficult.

"You think so? What if I make things even more complicated?" he asked.

Sarah placed a reassuring hand on his shoulder.

"Sometimes, being honest and vulnerable is the only way to resolve the complications. If you care about her, it's worth taking that risk," she said.

Liam nodded, appreciating Sarah's advice. He knew that he couldn't continue hiding his true feelings from Emma, and maybe, just maybe, being open with her would lead to a resolution they both needed. As Liam left the bar, he sent a message to Emma, asking her to meet him at a local park near her place. Emma, eagerly awaiting a chance to discuss her feelings with Liam, quickly agreed to meet.

Emma and Liam met at the park an hour later, its cozy ambiance providing the backdrop. Autumn leaves rustled in the gentle breeze, creating a serene atmosphere as they found a quiet bench.

Liam cleared his throat, breaking the uneasy silence that hung between them.

"Emma, we need to talk. About us."

Emma nodded, a mix of anticipation and apprehension in her eyes.

"Yeah, Liam, we do," she said.

Liam took a deep breath, his gaze sincere.

"Look, Emma, I've been doing some serious thinking. And I can't deny it anymore. I have feelings for you, and they are more than just friendship. I care about you, not just because of our kiss at the club. I... I like you, Emma," he said carefully.

Emma's eyes widened, and time seemed to stand still for a moment. The weight of Liam's confession hung in the air, and her heart raced as she processed his words.

Finally, she spoke, her voice soft but uncertain.

"Liam, I... I've been feeling the same way."

Liam's eyes widened in surprise, a mix of relief and excitement coloring his expression.

"You do?" he asked.

Emma nodded, a shy smile playing on her lips.

"Yeah, Liam. But I'm scared. I don't want to lose our friendship, and things have been so complicated lately," she said.

Liam reached for Emma's hand, squeezing it gently.

"Emma, I get it. I'm scared, too, but I can't ignore what I feel. Our friendship means the world to me, and I don't want to lose it either," Liam expressed. "But I can't keep pretending these feelings aren't there."

Tears welled up in Emma's eyes as she met Liam's gaze.

"Liam, I don't want to hurt you, and I don't want to be hurt either. But I can't deny that there's something between us. It's just... complicated," she told him.

"Emma, life is complicated, and feelings are messy. But I don't want to look back and wonder, 'What if.' We can figure this out together," said Liam, wiping away a tear from her cheek.

As they sat there, beginning to steer through the delicate territory between friendship and something more, the vulnerability of their emotions hung in the air. At that moment, they both realized that some feelings were too strong to be ignored, and the journey of exploring those emotions had only just begun.

Chapter 6: The Thorny Path of Truth

Emma's heart raced as she sat on a weathered bench, looking into Liam's eyes, her own filled with a mixture of excitement and love. Their emotions swirled like a tempest, and before they could overthink it, Liam leaned closer.

Their lips met in a tender, passionate kiss that sent shivers down their spines. Time stood still as they shared this electric moment, the park fading into the background. It was a kiss that changed everything, sealing their unspoken promises and igniting a new chapter in their relationship. As they pulled away, their eyes locked once more, a newfound sense of certainty filling their hearts.

The park, bathed in the soft, fading light, bore witness to the beginning of their romantic journey. It was a journey that had been years in the making, unfolding before them now in all its beautiful, promising glory. The soft glow of the streetlights cast a warm and inviting halo around them. Then, Liam broke the silence with a gentle smile.

"Emma, would you like a ride home?" he asked, his voice soft and sincere.

Emma looked at him, her heart warmed by his offer. In the past, she would have hesitated, preferring her independence. But tonight was different. Tonight, she gladly accepted his gesture.

"Thank you, Liam. I'd appreciate that," she replied, her smile mirroring his. Liam held the car door open for her, and she slid into the passenger seat. As he settled into the driver's seat, the engine purred to life, and they began their journey home.

The car glided smoothly through the quiet streets, the gentle hum of the engine creating a soothing backdrop to their conversation. They talked about everything and nothing, their words flowing effortlessly, as if they had known each other their whole lives.

The night air was cool and crisp, carrying with it a sense of serenity that wrapped around them like a warm touch. Liam's eyes flickered with affection as he stole glances at Emma, the moonlight highlighting the contours of her face. Liam drove safely, focused on the road ahead, but his heart was firmly entwined with Emma's. The world outside seemed to fade into the background as they continued to talk. The moment when they approached Emma's home was bittersweet.

The car rolled to a gentle stop outside Emma's apartment building. The night air held a hint of coolness, and the soft glow of the streetlights painted a cozy ambiance around them.

Liam turned off the engine and turned to Emma, his eyes filled with a mixture of excitement and uncertainty.

"Emma, about us..." he began, his voice tinged with hesitation.

Emma met his gaze, her heart racing.

"Liam, I feel it too," she admitted, her words carrying a sense of vulnerability.

Liam nodded, his fingers gently intertwining with hers.

"I don't want to rush into anything, Emma. I care about you so much, and I don't want to risk our friendship," he said softly.

"I understand, Liam. I feel the same way. Let's take things slow, one step at a time," said Emma, squeezing his hand reassuringly.

They both acknowledged the risks and uncertainties that lay ahead. However, their connection was undeniable, a feeling they couldn't ignore. Liam smiled, a sense of relief washing over him.

"I'm glad you feel that way. I want to get to know you on a deeper level, to explore what this could be," he said.

"Me too, Liam. I think we have something special, and I'm willing to see where it takes us," Emma replied, her eyes sparkling with anticipation.

With that mutual understanding, they sealed their unspoken pact with a tender kiss, a promise to go through this new chapter in their relationship with caution and care. The night around them seemed to hold its breath as if in anticipation of the journey ahead for Emma and Liam. It was one replete with hope, uncertainty, and the potential for a love story unlike any other.

***

Emma's phone chimed with Liam's sweet and romantic message as the sun cast a warm glow into her room the next morning. She couldn't help but blush as she read his words, feeling a rush of happiness.

"Good morning, Emma. I hope you have a wonderful day ahead," the message read.

"Good morning, Liam. You just made my day!" Emma quickly replied with a smile.

Overcome with a feeling of excitement, Emma got ready for work, humming a tune as she went about her morning routine. The prospect of exploring this budding romance with Liam filled her with a sense of anticipation.

At the busy workplace, the day progressed with the usual string of meetings, emails, and tasks. Liam and Emma had managed to maintain their professionalism, working side by side without letting their personal relationship interfere with their responsibilities.

As the clock ticked for their afternoon meeting, the two found themselves in a conference room with a handful of their colleagues. It revolved around the progress of their ongoing project, and Liam, known for his keen eye for detail, was reviewing the latest reports.

His voice filled the room as he addressed the team, his tone measured and focused. "Everything looks great so far, but I did notice a minor error in one of the reports," he pointed out, projecting the report onto the screen for everyone to see.

Emma's heart sank as she realized her mistake. She had worked tirelessly on the report, and the thought of an error slipping through made her cringe. Liam's criticism was fair, but it still stung.

Her colleagues nodded in agreement with Liam's assessment, and Emma couldn't help but feel a twinge of disappointment in herself. She had always prided herself on her attention to detail, and this oversight felt like a dent in her professional armor.

The meeting continued, and Liam moved on to other matters, but Emma couldn't shake the feeling of inadequacy that had washed over her. She kept her head down, determined to correct her mistake as soon as possible.

Ever perceptive, Liam noticed Emma's downcast expression. He understood the weight of perfectionism and the pressure she put on herself. So, he decided to reach out to her after the meeting.

"Hey, Emma," he typed on his computer, sending her a private message, "I hope I didn't upset you earlier. I just wanted to make sure everything is accurate."

Emma glanced at the message and quickly replied, "No, Liam, not at all. I appreciate your attention to detail. It's just me being hard on myself."

Liam's response was swift and reassuring. "I'm glad you understand. I didn't want to come across as too critical. We all make mistakes sometimes," it said.

Emma smiled as she read his message. It was a reminder that they were not just colleagues but also friends who cared about each other's well-being.

Their brief exchange lightened the atmosphere, and Emma's smile returned. As the workday drew to a close, Liam couldn't contain his excitement any longer. "Emma, are you free tonight? I was thinking maybe we could go out for dinner?" he told her.

Emma's heart skipped a beat as she read his message.

"Yes, Liam, I'd love to! Where should we meet?" she instantly replied.

Liam suggested a restaurant nearby, and they agreed on a time to meet later that evening. Emma couldn't help but feel a sense of happiness and anticipation, knowing that tonight would be their first official date. It was a step into the unknown, but one she was more than willing to take with Liam by her side.

The evening was set aglow by the soft, flickering candlelight as Emma and Liam sat at a cozy table in the charming restaurant. The warm, intimate ambiance created the perfect setting for their first official date.

As they perused the menu, their eyes occasionally met, and shy smiles passed between them. They were both a little nervous, but the moment's excitement far outweighed any anxiety. Liam reached across the table to pour a glass of wine for Emma, their fingers brushing ever so briefly, sending a delightful shiver through them both.

Emma's heart raced as she looked into Liam's eyes.

"This place is amazing, Liam. I'm so glad you brought me here," she told him.

"Emma, I wanted tonight to be special because you're special," Liam replied, his eyes widening.

Their conversation flowed effortlessly, filled with laughter and stories. They talked about their families, dreams, and favorite travel destinations. With each passing moment, they found themselves drawn closer, their connection growing stronger.

When their food arrived, they savored every bite, relishing the delicious flavors and the anticipation of what was building between them. Liam couldn't help but be captivated by Emma's animated storytelling. Meanwhile, Emma found herself enchanted by the way Liam's eyes lit up when he spoke about his architectural projects.

The candlelight danced in their eyes as the night deepened, adding an undeniably romantic touch to the atmosphere. They stole shy glances at each other, and their fingers occasionally brushed beneath the table, sending sparks of attraction between them.

"Liam, there's something about you that I can't quite put into words, but it's pulling me closer to you," Emma said softly, leaning closer.

"Emma, I feel it too. Being with you tonight feels like the most natural thing in the world," Liam replied, his heart racing.

Their dessert had arrived, but they were so engrossed in each other's company that they hardly noticed. The chemistry between them ignited, growing stronger with each stolen touch and lingering gaze.

When the evening came to an end, Liam drove Emma back to her apartment. The air between them was charged with magnetic tension. Neither of them was ready to say goodbye just yet. It was Emma who broke the silence, her voice soft and shy.

"Would you like to come upstairs for a while, Liam? I mean, if you want to..." she said.

Liam didn't need much convincing.

"I'd love to, Emma. A little more time with you sounds perfect," he replied with a charming smile.

They made their way upstairs to Emma's cozy apartment, their attraction palpable. She offered Liam a cup of coffee, an excuse to spend more time together. Liam chuckled, a playful glint in his eyes.

"Coffee at this hour? You're going to keep me up all night, Emma."

Emma's cheeks flushed as she realized the innuendo in his offer.

"I didn't mean... unless you want to stay up," she stammered, feeling a mix of embarrassment and excitement.

Liam's laughter was warm and genuine. "I'd stay up all night with you, Emma, no matter the reason," he said.

The conversation became more intimate as they sat on the couch with their coffee. They talked about their fears and dreams, baring their souls to each other. It was a connection that went beyond physical attraction; it was a meeting of minds and hearts.

As the hours passed, their desire became irresistible, their lips meeting in a passionate kiss. With Liam's lips on hers, Emma felt her body swoon into his. The taste of each other was intoxicating, and their bodies trembled with desire as they moved from the coffee table to the floor, their kisses growing more fervent and urgent.

In a daze of emotions and longing, they stumbled into Emma's bedroom, the world outside fading away as they gave in to their impulses. Emma was glad that the room was dark. Liam hadn't turned any lights on; the only illumination came from outside the window.

Liam's hands traced Emma's delicate skin as he kissed down her neck and onto her shoulder, slipping down her top so her skin was bare against his lips.

Emma's hand ran through his silky hair and then over his back. The heat of his skin and the muscles of his back gave Emma a shivery feeling in the pit of her stomach. She was immersed in the scent of Liam's body, unaware of her clothes slipping off. Liam's grip across her waist got stronger yet gentle enough not to hurt her.

In that intimate moment, Liam gently pushed Emma towards the bed, pushing her down against the silk covers. Despite the darkness, Emma could see the lingering intensity. Soon, Liam's lips were on hers again, passionately kissing her. Their first night together was a whirlwind of sensations, their bodies pressed close, their hearts racing.

Their emotions ran high as they felt excited and nervous about taking their relationship to the next stage. Their love story took a passionate turn as they lay entwined in each other's arms. They knew that this was just the beginning of their relationship.

Chapter 7: Exploring Love

The city was still and serene in the early hours of a Saturday morning. Emma's balcony was filled with nothing but the soft melody of birdsong; there wasn't even a whisper of traffic or the hustle and bustle of crowds to be heard. She unfurled her yoga mat, its soft fabric uncoiling like a ribbon. Hannah was there to accompany Emma in her morning routine.

The sun peeked over the rooftops, casting a warm glow over the two friends as they stretched and breathed in sync with the rising day. The air was crisp and clean, with a hint of dew lingering from the previous night. As they moved through their poses, Emma couldn't contain her excitement, eager to share her recent experience with Hannah.

"Hannah, you won't believe what happened last night," Emma said, her voice filled with excitement.

Hannah raised an eyebrow, intrigued. "What happened? Tell me," she replied, mirroring Emma's downward dog pose.

With a smile, Emma began recounting the events of the previous evening, her words flowing effortlessly as she described her intimate night with Liam. The tender moments, the kisses, the overwhelming emotions – she shared it all with her best friend, her voice tinged with joy and affection.

Just as Emma finished her story, her phone buzzed, interrupting their conversation. She reached over to check the notification, a playful grin spreading across her face as she read the message.

"It's Liam," she announced, excitement evident in her voice. "He's asking if I'm free tomorrow."

Hannah chuckled, a knowing smile on her lips. "Looks like someone's eager to see you again," she teased, a hint of mischief in her tone. Emma blushed, her heart fluttering at the thought of spending more time with Liam. She returned to her phone to quickly type, "Yes, I'm free."

"Great! How about we go on an adventure this weekend? I've got something special planned for us," they replied.

Excitement bubbled up inside Emma as she read his words, her mind already racing with possibilities. With a smile spreading across her face, she quickly replied, "Sounds intriguing! I'm definitely up for an adventure. What did you have in mind?"

Liam's response came swiftly, filled with anticipation. "It's a surprise! Just pack a bag and meet me at the park tomorrow morning. I promise you won't be disappointed," he wrote.

The rest of the day felt like a whirlwind of excitement for Emma. With every passing hour, her anticipation for the upcoming adventure with Liam grew stronger. She couldn't help but feel a flutter of nerves as she imagined what surprises he had in store for her.

Each task she completed was tinged with the thrill of the unknown, and she found herself practically bouncing with excitement. Time seemed to drag on endlessly as she counted the minutes until their meeting at the park. Despite her attempts to focus on other things, her mind kept drifting back to Liam and the promise of an unforgettable day ahead.

Emma arrived at the park the following day, her heart pounding with excitement as she scanned the area for any sign of Liam. Suddenly, she spotted him standing near a charming vintage jeep, a broad grin on his face.

"Hey there, ready for our adventure?" Liam called out, his eyes twinkling with mischief.

Emma's excitement grew as she approached him, her curiosity piqued by the sight of the open-roofed jeep. "Absolutely! But you're going to have to give me a hint about what's in store," she teased.

Liam chuckled, offering her a playful wink. "No hints, I'm afraid. You'll just have to trust me and enjoy the ride," he said. With a sense of anticipation coursing through her veins, Emma climbed into the jeep beside Liam, the door closing with a soft click behind her.

The breeze tousled their hair as they cruised along in the jeep. Emma glanced up, taking in the vast expanse of sky above them, dotted with fluffy white clouds. Liam grinned, his eyes alight with excitement as they ventured further into the wilderness. As they journeyed through the picturesque countryside, Emma couldn't contain her awe at the stunning landscapes passing by. "Wow, Liam, this place is incredible!" she exclaimed, her eyes wide with wonder.

Liam chuckled, glancing over at Emma with a fond smile. "I'm glad you like it. This spot has always been one of my favorites," he replied, his voice filled with warmth.

Emma leaned back in her seat, feeling utterly content as they continued their drive. "So, tell me, Liam, do you have any funny stories from your early days in professional life?" she asked, a playful grin tugging at her lips.

Liam chuckled, recalling a particularly memorable moment. "Oh, I've got one for you," he said, his eyes sparkling with amusement. "Back when I was just starting out, I had this big presentation to give to some important clients. I was so nervous that I accidentally spilled coffee all over my shirt right before I went on stage!"

Emma burst into laughter at the mental image, imagining Liam frantically trying to clean up the mess. "No way! What did you do then?" she asked, barely able to contain her amusement.

Liam shrugged, a sheepish grin spreading across his face. "Well, I had no choice but to roll with it. I just made a joke about it during my presentation and hoped for the best," he admitted.

"And did it work?" Emma asked, her curiosity piqued.

Liam nodded, a hint of pride in his voice. "Surprisingly, yes! The clients loved it and even complimented me on my ability to stay calm under pressure," he replied, a smile of satisfaction tugging at his lips.

Emma grinned, feeling a surge of affection for Liam as she listened to his story. "You never cease to impress me, Liam," she said, reaching over to squeeze his hand gently. "Thanks for sharing that with me."

Hours later, they arrived at their destination: a secluded cabin located deep in the heart of the woods. Emma's eyes widened in awe as she took in the picturesque surroundings, the beautiful lake shimmering in the afternoon sun. "This is incredible, Liam! I never would have guessed," Emma exclaimed, her heart overflowing with gratitude.

Liam grinned, his eyes shining with happiness. "I wanted to create a special memory for us, something we'll always treasure," he said. As they stepped inside the cozy cabin, a sense of awe washed over Emma. The interior was adorned with rustic charm, and the walls were made of weathered wood and with twinkling fairy lights. A soft, plush couch sat in the center of the room, with plush cushions and warm blankets, inviting them to sink into its comfort.

Against one wall, a large bed beckoned with its soft, inviting sheets and fluffy pillows. The flickering glow of candles cast a warm, intimate ambiance, filling the space with a soft, golden light. A small wooden table stood nearby, filled with delicious snacks and refreshments, inviting them to indulge in a leisurely feast.

In the corner of the room, a projector whirred quietly, casting a soft glow on the opposite wall. A stack of DVDs lay nearby, offering a selection of movies for them to enjoy together. Liam gestured toward the makeshift theater setup with a smile.

"I thought we could watch a movie later if you'd like," he suggested, his eyes sparkling with excitement. Emma's heart swelled with affection as she took in the thoughtful details of their cozy retreat. "I'd love that," she replied, her voice filled with warmth. "Thank you, Liam. This is truly wonderful."

With a contented smile, Liam led Emma further into the cabin, eager to show her the rest of their romantic getaway. As they explored their temporary home, the scent of pine and woodsmoke filled the air, enveloping them in a sense of serenity and peace.

As Liam led Emma deeper into the cabin, their fingers intertwined, a wave of warmth and affection washed over them. In a moment of unspoken understanding, they paused, their eyes meeting in a silent exchange of love and longing. Without a word, Liam gently cupped Emma's face in his hands, his touch tender and reverent.

Leaning in closer, their breath mingled in the air, their hearts beating in perfect harmony. And then, in a rush of emotion, their lips met in a soft, sweet kiss. It was a kiss filled with promise and passion, a testament to the deep connection they shared.

As they pulled away, their eyes locked in a silent exchange of love and devotion. In that fleeting moment, amidst the flickering candlelight and the soft glow of the cabin, Emma knew that she was exactly where she was meant to be – in Liam's arms, surrounded by love and warmth.

With the sun hanging low in the sky, Liam and Emma set off to explore the enchanting woods surrounding their cozy cabin. Hand in hand, they wandered along winding paths, the earthy scent of pine filling the air as they immersed themselves in the beauty of nature.

They walked by towering trees, their branches reaching toward the sky like outstretched arms, and listened to the gentle rustle of leaves as a soft breeze whispered through the forest. Emma's laughter echoed through the woods as they stumbled upon a hidden clearing, bathed in dappled sunlight filtering through the dense canopy above. They paused to take in the breathtaking beauty of their surroundings, the serene silence broken only by the distant calls of woodland creatures.

"Look at that big tree!" Emma exclaimed, pointing at a massive oak. Liam chuckled, "It's like something out of a storybook, isn't it?" They laughed and continued their stroll, soaking in the peacefulness around them.

After a while, Emma noticed the sun starting to dip low in the sky. "I think it's getting late, Liam. Maybe we should head back to the cabin," she suggested. Liam nodded, "You're right. We don't want to get lost in the dark!" They made their way back, chatting about their favorite parts of the forest adventure.

As they approached the cabin, Liam glanced up at the darkening sky. "Looks like it's going to be a starry night," he remarked. Emma smiled, "Perfect for cozying up by the fire." They stepped inside, feeling grateful for the warmth and comfort awaiting them after their woodland exploration.

* * *

The evening descended, and the fire crackled in the cabin's fireplace, casting dancing shadows across the cozy room; Emma and Liam found themselves drawn to each other like moths to a flame.

With a playful twinkle in his eye, Liam leaned closer to Emma, his voice low and husky. "You know, Emma, I never would have guessed that our adventure would lead us to a place like this," he said, a mischievous grin playing on his lips.

Emma laughed softly, her eyes sparkling with amusement. "Well, I have to admit, you do have a knack for surprises," she replied, her tone teasing.

Leaning in even closer, Liam brushed a stray lock of hair from Emma's face, his touch sending shivers down her spine. "But you know what they say, Emma. The best adventures are the ones we least expect," he murmured, his voice filled with warmth and affection.

Emma's heart fluttered at Liam's words, her cheeks flushing with color. "I couldn't agree more," she whispered, her voice barely above a breath.

As they gazed into each other's eyes, the crackling fire casting a warm glow around them, Emma felt a surge of love and longing wash over her.

***

Emma blinked as the sunlight filtered through the window, gently nudging her awake. Liam was already up, sitting beside her with a tender smile. "Good morning, sleepyhead," he greeted, his eyes full of adoration.

Blushing, Emma sat up, feeling a warmth spread through her cheeks. "What?" she asked, a hint of shyness in her voice.

Liam reached out to tuck a loose strand of hair behind her ear. "You're just so beautiful," he whispered before placing a soft kiss on her forehead.

As they packed their belongings and prepared to leave the cabin, Emma turned to Liam with a grateful smile. "I can't thank you enough for this weekend, Liam. It was perfect," she said, her eyes shining with sincerity.

Liam took her hand in his, squeezing it gently. "I'm glad you enjoyed it, Emma. Being here with you has meant everything to me," he replied, his voice filled with warmth.

As they drove back to the city, their conversation flowed effortlessly, reflecting the deep connection they had forged during their time together. They spoke of their hopes, dreams, and fears, sharing their innermost thoughts with each other without reservation.

As they drove through the winding roads back to the city, Emma couldn't help but feel a sense of contentment wash over her. Leaning back in her seat, she turned to Liam with a soft smile. "You know, Liam, I've never felt so at peace as I do right now," she said, her voice filled with sincerity.

Liam glanced over at her, his eyes sparkling with affection. "I feel the same way, Emma. Being with you feels like coming home," he replied, his hand finding hers on the gearshift.

Emma's heart fluttered at his words, a warm sensation spreading through her chest. "It's funny how life works sometimes," she mused, her gaze drifting out the window to the passing scenery. "I never imagined that a weekend getaway would lead to something so beautiful."

Liam squeezed her hand gently, his thumb tracing circles on her skin. "Me neither, Emma. But I'm grateful for every moment we've shared," he said, his voice soft yet filled with conviction. "And I can't wait to see what the future holds for us."

Through their words and actions, it was clear that they had learned to trust and love again, overcoming past hurts and insecurities. With open hearts and minds, they embraced the future that lay ahead, knowing that together, they could conquer anything that came their way.

Chapter 8: Love's Battlefield

The clock struck midnight. The office was awash in a muted, orange glow from the overhead lamp, casting long shadows on the walls and floor. The dim lighting accentuated the clutter on Emma's desk, a disarray of papers and stacked folders. Her computer screen was the brightest spot in the room, constantly changing with the influx of emails.

Emma's eyelids drooped, heavy with exhaustion, the weight of a long day settling in on her. However, her heart fluttered with anticipation as she eagerly awaited Liam's message. Suddenly, the dull buzz of her phone shattered the silence around her, and Liam's voice filled her ears.

The disappointment in his tone was palpable as he spoke.

"I'm sorry, Emma. I know we had movie plans tonight, but I'm stuck at a meeting with an international client. It's taking longer than expected."

She could almost see him rubbing his tired eyes and running his fingers through his hair in frustration.

The distant sound of papers rustling and phones ringing echoed in the background, evidence of his hectic work environment. A pang of sympathy mixed with disappointment washed over Emma as she realized their date would have to be postponed yet again.

Emma sighed, her shoulders slumping with resignation.

"It's okay, Liam. I understand," she replied, trying to sound more composed than she felt. "We'll just have to reschedule."

They had been looking forward to this date for weeks, a rare opportunity to unwind and reconnect away from the stresses of work. But as deadlines loomed and responsibilities piled up, their demanding schedules repeatedly derailed their plans.

"I promise we'll make it up to each other," Liam reassured her, his voice tinged with regret. "I miss you, Emma."

"I miss you too," Emma whispered, her heart heavy with longing. "We'll figure this out, Liam. I know we will."

They hung up the phone, but Emma couldn't shake the nagging disappointment lingering in the air. Despite their best intentions, their relationship was beginning to feel the strain of their busy lives. With a heavy heart, she gathered her belongings and made her way to the exit.

Outside, the alleyway was cloaked in darkness, the only illumination coming from the faint glow of the streetlights. Emma hugged her coat tighter around her, feeling a shiver run down her spine as she stepped into the chilly night air.

Her footsteps echoed softly against the pavement as she walked, the sound muffled by the silence of the empty street. But as she turned a corner, a sudden sense of unease washed over her, prickling at the back of her neck.

Emma quickened her pace, her heart pounding and senses on high alert. Every shadow seemed to loom larger, every sound more ominous. She couldn't shake the feeling that someone – or something – was following her.

With a gasp, Emma broke into a run, her pulse racing as she darted through the deserted streets. But in her haste, she failed to see the small stone lying in her path, and with a cry of pain, she stumbled and fell, scraping her elbow on the rough pavement.

As she lay there, nursing her bruised ego more than anything else, a voice cut through the darkness. It was an old man with a weathered and kind face standing nearby with a look of concern.

"Are you alright, miss?" he asked, his voice gentle and reassuring.

Emma nodded, forcing a shaky smile.

"I'm fine, thank you," she replied, her voice trembling slightly. "Just a little shaken."

The old man offered her a hand, helping her to her feet with a reassuring smile.

"Take care now," he said, his voice fading into the night as Emma stopped a passing taxi. As she climbed into the backseat, Emma couldn't shake the feeling of anger that simmered beneath the surface. She dialed Hannah's number, her fingers trembling as she typed out a message.

"Can I sleep over at your place tonight?" she whispered as she wrote, her voice thick with frustration and distress.

As the taxi pulled away into the night, Emma's thoughts turned to Liam, her anger growing with every passing moment. How could he leave her alone late in the night? And more importantly, would their relationship work out like this?

Emma's frustration was palpable when she stormed into Hannah's apartment. Sensing her friend's anguish, Hannah immediately recognized something was amiss.

"Emma, what's wrong?" Hannah asked, her brow furrowing with concern as she watched Emma pace back and forth across the room. Emma let out a frustrated sigh, sinking onto the couch beside Hannah.

"It's Liam," she confessed, her voice tinged with disappointment. "He called off our movie night plans at the last moment."

Hannah's eyes widened in surprise. "Really? That's unlike him," she remarked, her tone filled with sympathy.

Emma nodded, her anger bubbling to the surface. "I know, right? It's like we can never seem to find time for each other anymore," she lamented, her voice tinged with sadness.

Hannah reached out, placing a comforting hand on Emma's shoulder. "I'm sorry, Em. It sounds like you guys are really struggling with your schedules," she said, her voice gentle and understanding.

Emma nodded, her eyes welling with tears.

"It's just so hard. We barely get to see each other anymore, and when we do, it feels like we're always rushing to catch up," she confessed, her voice choked with emotion.

"I know it's tough, but you guys will get through this. You just need to communicate and make time for each other, even if it's just for a few minutes each day," Hannah said, reassuringly squeezing Emma's hand.

Emma nodded, a small smile tugging at the corners of her lips.

"You're right, Hannah. Thanks for being here for me," she said.

They talked late into the night, and Emma felt as if a weight had been lifted off her shoulders.

However, Liam and Emma became increasingly caught in a whirlwind of conflicting schedules and mounting work pressures in the following months. Despite their best intentions, they struggled to align their calendars and make time for each other. As a result, many of their plans were called off, leaving them feeling ever more disconnected and distant.

Their relationship began to falter under the weight of their demanding careers, as they found themselves trapped in a cycle of missed opportunities and unmet expectations. With each canceled date and postponed outing, the gap between them seemed to widen, leaving them both feeling frustrated and alone.

Emma had been looking forward to a romantic dinner with Liam at their favorite restaurant one evening. She had been eagerly anticipating spending quality time together, hoping to reconnect after yet another hectic week. However, as the evening approached, Liam called to cancel their plans at the last minute, citing a work meeting that had suddenly come up.

Disgruntled by yet another canceled date, Emma couldn't help but express her disappointment to Liam when they met the next day. She voiced her feelings, explaining how she had been looking forward to their time together and how his constant work commitments were starting to take a toll on their relationship.

"Liam, I can't believe you canceled on me again! I've been looking forward to this all week, and now you're telling me you must work late. It's not fair!"

"I'm sorry, Emma, but I had no choice. The meeting ran longer than expected, and I couldn't just walk out. You know how important this project is for my career," Liam sighed, running a hand through his disheveled hair.

Emma's frustration bubbled to the surface, her voice tinged with emotion.

"But what about us? What about our relationship? It feels like you always put work first, and I'm tired of feeling like I'm not a priority."

Her words hung heavy in the air, and the tension between them was palpable as they stood on opposite sides of the room. Liam's jaw clenched, his voice slightly rising as he struggled to explain himself.

"That's not fair, Emma," Liam retorted, his tone defensive. "You know how much importance this deal holds for my business. I'm doing my best, but it's never enough for you."

Emma's eyes flashed with anger and hurt, her voice slightly trembling as she spoke.

"It's just about spending time with each other. I want quality time. I want us to make memories. But it seems like you'd rather be at work than with me."

Their voices grew louder, each word adding fuel to the fire of their argument. Despite their love for each other, they struggled to find common ground, their differing perspectives driving them further apart.

For a whole week, silence hung heavily between Emma and Liam, each day feeling longer and emptier without their usual conversations and laughter. Liam knew he had to do something to fix things, to bridge the growing gap between them. With a determination born out of love, he enlisted the help of Emma's friend Hannah to plan a special surprise.

On a crisp Saturday morning, Hannah arrived at Emma's doorstep with a mischievous glint in her eye.

"Come on, Emma, I've got something amazing planned for you!" she exclaimed, practically bouncing with excitement.

Surprised and curious, Emma followed Hannah to the park, where she found Liam waiting with a picnic basket filled with Emma's favorite foods and a bouquet of her favorite flowers. Emma's eyes widened in surprise as she took in the scene before her. Meanwhile, Liam stood there with a sheepish smile, holding out his hand to her.

"I'm sorry, Emma," he said softly, his voice tinged with sincerity. "I know I haven't been the best lately, but I want to make it up to you. Will you give me another chance?"

Emma felt a rush of emotions wash over her — surprise, gratitude, and, above all, love. Tears welled up in her eyes as she nodded, unable to find the words to express how she felt.

Liam pulled her into a warm embrace, holding her tightly as if never wanting to let her go.

From then on, Emma and Liam's relationship began to recover. They made sure to spend time together even with their busy schedules. True to his commitment to make it up to Emma, Liam planned a two-week trip through Europe, including all the places he knew she would love. He poured over guidebooks in his spare time, meticulously scheduling flights, trains, and hotel reservations in Rome, Venice, Lucerne, and beyond. Once all the preparations were made, Liam could no longer contain his excitement.

"Guess what, Emma? I've planned a surprise trip for us to Europe!" he told Emma with a sparkle in his eyes.

Emma's eyes widened with excitement, and she couldn't help but let out a squeal of delight.

"Europe? Oh my goodness, Liam, that's amazing!" she exclaimed, jumping up from the couch and wrapping her arms around him.

Their anticipation only grew as they hastily packed their bags and tied up loose ends at work. Finally, the day arrived, and they boarded the plane hand in hand, ready for an adventure of a lifetime. As soon as the plane touched down in Rome, Liam squeezed Emma's hand in excitement.

"We're finally here!" he told her with a smile.

As they walked through the airport terminal, Emma took in the sights and sounds of the bustling city.

"Where to first?" she asked Liam.

"I thought we could start at the Spanish Steps. Then maybe grab a slice of pizza to share," he replied.

Soon, they emerged hand in hand from the metro station into the warm Roman sunlight. They were greeted by the sight of ancient architecture lining the narrow streets and locals and tourists walking along the sidewalks.

Liam pointed out landmarks like the Colosseum in the distance as they ate their pizza overlooking the city.

"It's so romantic here," Emma sighed, resting her head on his shoulder.

That evening, Liam made a reservation at a rooftop restaurant with views of the illuminated city. They talked and laughed for hours over bottles of Aglianico wine. When a guitarist started playing love songs, Liam took Emma's hand, and they slowly danced under the stars.

The next day, they took the train to Venice. After checking into their hotel, Liam suggested exploring the city's waterways by gondola. As they floated past elegant palazzos and bridges, Emma couldn't help but be a little mesmerized.

"This place is like something out of a dream!" she exclaimed.

At night, they strolled through lively St. Mark's Square and ate seafood risotto at a charming bacaro.

After spending a few similarly blissful days in Venice, Liam and Emma boarded a train bound for Switzerland. Emma gasped at the natural beauty as soon as the snow-capped Alps came into view. They arrived in Lucerne late afternoon and checked into a cozy hotel overlooking the lake.

Later that evening, Liam surprised Emma with tickets to see the Lion Monument illuminated after dark. The famous lions glowed a warm yellow against the twilight as the sun set over the mountains. Then, Liam led Emma down a tree-lined path lit with lanterns. They arrived at a secluded waterfront restaurant, where a private table had been arranged overlooking the lake.

They fed each other bites of fondue and sipped full-bodied merlot in a four-course meal of Swiss specialties. Liam pulled Emma close as the moon rose over the dance floor while a live band played Waltzes. They slowly twirled under the stars, lost in each other's eyes. Afterward, on the walk back to their hotel, Emma thanked Liam with a lingering kiss.

"This has been the most perfect night," she sighed.

The next morning, they took the cable car up Mount Pilatus for breathtaking panoramic views. Unbeknownst to Emma, Liam had a very special surprise planned for her when they reached the top of Mount Pilatus. As the cable car rose higher, allowing more spectacular views of green hills and snowy peaks, he grew increasingly nervous with anticipation.

When they finally stepped off at the summit, Emma's phone rang. She glanced at the screen, and her heart skipped a beat - it was a call from her dream company in Paris. Hands shaking, she answered the call to find out she'd gotten the job.

A surge of excitement coursed through her veins as she imagined herself strolling along the cobblestone streets of Montmartre, sipping espresso at quaint sidewalk cafes, and admiring the breathtaking views from the Eiffel Tower. This was the chance she had been waiting for, the opportunity to turn her dreams into reality.

With a broad smile, she rushed to share the news with Liam.

"Liam, you won't believe it! I just got a job offer to work overseas - in Paris!" Emma exclaimed, her voice filled with joy.

Liam's expression shifted from curiosity to surprise, then quickly to anger.

"Paris? You're moving to Paris? When did you apply for the job? Why don't I know anything about it?" he exclaimed, his voice rising with each word.

Emma winced at the intensity of his reaction, trying to explain.

"I didn't mean to keep it from you, Liam. It's just... it all happened so fast, and I wanted to make sure it was real before I said anything."

Liam's anger softened into sadness as he realized the implications of Emma's decision.

"But Emma, what about us? What about our relationship? How can you just leave like this?" he asked.

Tears welled up in Emma's eyes as she struggled to find the right words.

"Liam, I... I don't want to leave you. But this is an incredible opportunity for me, something I've always dreamed of. Please try to understand."

Liam sighed, his shoulders slumping in defeat.

"I do understand, Emma. And I want what's best for you. It's just... it's going to be hard for me, knowing you're so far away," he said dejectedly, his hand reaching into his pocket that held the surprise he had for her - a ring.

While Liam's finger traced the small velvet box in contemplation, Emma reached out and took his hand. Something in him decided against taking out the box then.

"I know, Liam. And I promise I'll do everything I can to make this work. We'll figure it out together, okay?" Emma said, squeezing Liam's hand gently.

With a heavy heart, Liam nodded, silently resigning himself to the reality of Emma's decision. Deep down, he knew that saying goodbye wouldn't be easy. After a long, silent embrace with tears streaming down their cheeks, they made their way back down the mountain.

In the busy weeks leading up to Emma's move to Paris, she and Liam remained busy. Emma had lots of things to do, like pack up her stuff and say goodbye to her friends. However, Liam was there to help her with everything, as always.

Together, they went through all of Emma's things, deciding what to keep and get rid of. As it turned out, Liam was really good at staying calm and helping Emma stay organized, which was super helpful. He even helped her figure out all the paperwork she needed for her new job in Paris.

Chapter 9: Weathering the Storms Together

Liam's head was buried in work on a particularly chaotic afternoon, his mind consumed with endless tasks and deadlines. Suddenly, the shrill sound of his phone ringing broke through the hustle and bustle. He reached for it, seeing Emma's name flash across the screen.

"Hey, Liam!" her voice rang like a soothing balm, cutting through the noise and calming Liam's frantic state. "I was wondering if you would like to come shopping with me? I could use your opinion on some outfits."

Liam's heart warmed at the invitation.

"Of course, Emma! I'd love to join you," he replied, his voice full of enthusiasm.

The designated spot was a small, quaint square amid the lively city of San Francisco. Emma arrived first, wearing a striking yellow strapped dress that hugged her curves. As Liam pulled up in his car, he couldn't help but be mesmerized by her beauty. He knew this sight would soon be out of his reach, as their time together dwindled.

"Hey," Emma waved, making Liam's heart skip a beat.

"I hope I didn't keep you waiting," he said, rushing to her side and taking her hand in his.

"No, I just got here," Emma said, smiling warmly at him before leading him toward the charming winter clothing shop she had wanted to explore.

As she stepped inside the shop, Emma's eyes widened in delight at the rows of garments hanging before her. Her gaze eagerly roamed over each rack, taking in the striking colors and intricate designs. Suddenly, a beautiful dress caught her eye, its delicate lace and flowing fabric almost beckoning to her.

"Liam, come see this!" she exclaimed, holding it up for him to admire. "It's like something out of a fairytale."

Liam's warm smile deepened as he took in the sight of Emma, surrounded by the whimsical attire.

"It's perfect," he whispered, his voice full of love and admiration. "Just like you."

The soft light filtering through the windows seemed to glow even brighter with their presence, casting an enchanting aura over the scene.

Emma blushed at his words, feeling warmth wash over her.

"You think so?"

Liam nodded, his heart swelling with love.

"Absolutely. And besides, it'll help you remember me when you're in Paris," he added, reaching for the dress and handing it to her. Emma's eyes widened in surprise as she took the dress from him.

"Liam, I don't need anything to remember you," she replied softly, her voice filled with emotion.

"I know, Emma. But it's just a little something to remind you of me," Liam said, his eyes shining with love.

Emma rushed into his embrace, feeling a surge of gratitude and love for the man standing before her.

"Thank you, Liam," she whispered, her heart overflowing with happiness.

Liam pulled her close, his arms wrapping around her as he pressed a tender kiss to her lips. At that moment, surrounded by the warmth and love of each other's embrace, they knew their love would endure no matter where life took them.

With their hearts content, they spent the rest of the afternoon trying on clothes and laughing together. It was indeed a nice break from all the stress of moving, and Emma was grateful to have Liam there with her.

"Thanks for today, Liam. I appreciate you being here for me," Emma said, turning to Liam as they exited a shop.

"I wouldn't want to be anywhere else," he said, smiling as he hugged her tightly. "Let's make the most of our time together."

***

The night before Emma's departure, Liam arrived at her apartment with a heavy heart, knowing that their time together was drawing to a close. He found Emma busy packing her luggage, her movements quick and efficient while she sorted through her belongings. He hesitated for a moment before stepping forward to offer his help.

"Do you need a hand with that?" he asked softly, his voice tinged with sadness.

Emma looked up, her eyes meeting Liam's with a mixture of gratitude and sorrow.

"I would appreciate that, thank you," she replied, her voice barely above a whisper.

Together, they worked in silence, the rustling of clothes and the occasional sigh the only sound in the room. Liam's hands moved with precision, folding each garment with care and placing it gently into Emma's suitcase.

Despite his efforts to remain composed, his sensitivity was palpable. His movements were slow and deliberate, as if trying to prolong their time together. Emma watched him quietly, her heart heavy with the weight of their impending separation.

As they finished packing, Liam turned to Emma, his eyes filled with sadness and resignation.

"I know you'll have an amazing time in Paris, Emma. But just remember to stay safe and take care of yourself," he said gently, his voice tinged with emotion.

Emma nodded, her eyes glistening with unshed tears.

"I will, Liam. You, too, take care of yourself," she replied, kissing him tenderly.

With heavy hearts, they made their way to the bedroom, where they settled down for the night. Liam wrapped his arms around Emma, holding her close as they drifted off to sleep, cherishing every precious moment they had left together before the dawn of a new chapter in Emma's life.

The morning sun rose all too soon, bathing the bedroom in a soft glow. Liam awoke first, not wanting to miss a moment of their last hours together. Careful not to disturb Emma's slumber, he slipped from the bed and into the kitchen. Knowing they were her favorite, Liam set about making crepes from scratch, whisking the batter to a silky smooth consistency. While the savory crepes sizzled on the griddle, filling the apartment with an enticing aroma, he began brewing a pot of strong coffee.

By the time Emma emerged from the bedroom, still beautiful despite tired eyes, the table was set with fluffy crepes, fresh berries, and steaming mugs.

"Bonjour mon amour," Liam said, greeting her with a kiss. "I wanted to treat you to a little taste of Paris before you go."

Over the home-cooked breakfast, they savored each remaining moment they had together. Though their hearts were heavy with sadness, their love and commitment to each other's dreams gave them hope that this separation would only make their reunion sweeter. All too soon, it was time for Emma to leave.

"I'll miss you, Emma," Liam said tenderly, his voice barely above a whisper.

Tears welled up in Emma's eyes as she stepped closer to him, wrapping her arms around him in a tight embrace.

"I'll miss you too, Liam," she whispered, her voice choked with emotion. They simply stood there for a moment, holding onto each other as if they could stop time itself. But eventually, they had to let go, knowing their time together was running out.

Liam drove Emma to the airport in silence, the weight of their impending goodbye hanging heavy in the air. The city passed by in a blur outside the car window, streetlights flickering like distant stars in the night sky. Emma glanced over at Liam occasionally, her heart aching with the realization that this would be the last time they would be together for a while.

When they reached the airport, Liam helped Emma unload her luggage from the car, each of his movements weighed down by the heaviness of Emma's looming departure. Emma's eyes glistened with unshed tears as she turned to face Liam, her heart aching at the thought of leaving him behind.

As their eyes locked in a silent exchange of love and longing, each second stretched as if time itself had slowed to a crawl. And then, unable to bear the weight of their emotions any longer, they closed the distance between them, their lips meeting in a tender, bittersweet kiss.

It was a kiss filled with love and sorrow, a silent farewell to the life they had shared until now. As they pulled away, their hearts were heavy with the burden their parting had inflicted on them.

***

Emma's heart fluttered with excitement as she stepped off the plane at Charles de Gaulle airport, her eyes taking in the surroundings of the busy airport. When she reached the arrival lounge, she was greeted by a tall, dark-haired man holding a sign with her name.

"Bonjour, I'm Pierre," he said with a warm smile, extending his hand in greeting. "Welcome to Paris!"

Emma returned his smile, feeling a sense of relief wash over her at the sight of a friendly face in this unfamiliar city.

"Thank you, Pierre," she replied, shaking his hand. "It's a pleasure to meet you." As they made their way into the city,

Pierre pointed out various landmarks along the way, regaling Emma with tales of life in Paris.

"This is the Eiffel Tower," he explained, gesturing towards the iconic structure looming in the distance.

"And over there is the Louvre, home to some of the world's most famous works of art."

Emma listened intently, her eyes wide with wonder as Pierre spoke. His fluent English and charming personality comforted her a little, easing some of the nerves she felt about starting her new job in a foreign country. "You've been in Paris for a while?" asked Emma, her curiosity piqued.

Pierre hesitated for a moment before replying, "Yes, that's correct."

As they drove through the lively streets of Paris, Emma couldn't help but feel a sense of excitement building within her — the beginning of a new adventure in the city of lights.

Soon, Pierre led Emma to her new apartment in a charming building with wrought-iron balconies and ivy-covered walls. As they climbed the stairs to the top floor, Emma couldn't help but feel a sense of exhilaration at the prospect of living in such a picturesque neighborhood.

The apartment was cozy yet elegant, with hardwood floors, high ceilings, and large windows that flooded the space with natural light. Pierre showed Emma around, pointing out the various amenities and making sure she felt comfortable in her new home.

"Here is your bedroom, and this is the living room," Pierre explained, his voice warm and reassuring. "And over here is the kitchen, where you can prepare your meals."

As Emma settled into her new surroundings, she couldn't help but feel nervous about starting her new job the next day. It was followed by a sudden thought of Liam, which brought a smile to her face. She dialed his number, eagerly anticipating hearing his voice on the other end of the line.

"Liam, you won't believe how amazing Paris is!" Emma exclaimed, her excitement palpable through the phone.

Liam listened intently, his heart swelling with a mixture of emotions. Pride washed over him as he heard about Emma's excitement and her positive experience in the new city.

"And let me tell you about Pierre, my liaison at the company," Emma added enthusiastically. "He's been an absolute lifesaver! He received me from the airport, gave me a brief tour around the city, and has been helping me get settled in. I don't know what I would do without him!"

Liam chuckled on the other end of the line.

"Should I be worried about this Pierre character stealing you away from me?" he teased, his voice tinged with playful jealousy.

Emma laughed, shaking her head.

"Oh, don't be silly, Liam. Pierre is just a friend and colleague. You have nothing to worry about," she reassured him, her tone warm and affectionate.

After a few more minutes of chatting and catching up, they said their goodbyes and hung up the call, both feeling reassured and connected despite the distance between them.

The next morning, Pierre arrived promptly at Emma's doorstep, a warm smile gracing his features as he greeted her. "Bonjour, Emma! Ready for the first day at work?" he asked cheerfully, holding the door open for her.

Getting into the car, Emma couldn't help but feel a pang of guilt for inconveniencing Pierre with her constant need for assistance. "I'm sorry for all the trouble I'm causing you," she said, her tone apologetic.

Pierre waved off her concerns with a gracious smile.

"Nonsense, Emma. It's my pleasure to help you settle in. Consider it a part of my job," he replied, his voice laced with sincerity.

During the ride to the office, Emma opened up to Pierre about her life back home, sharing stories about her family, friends, and of course, Liam. Pierre listened attentively, his eyes focused on the road, but his ears tuned to Emma's words.

"It sounds like you have a wonderful support system back home," Pierre remarked, his tone warm and encouraging.

Emma nodded, a small smile playing on her lips.

"Yes, I'm very lucky," she agreed. "Liam has been my rock through everything, and I don't know what I would do without him."

Pierre's expression shifted subtly, a fleeting shadow passing over his features before he composed himself. "It's clear how much he means to you," he said gently. "But don't worry, Emma. You're not alone here. I'll do everything I can to help you feel at home in Paris."

Soon, they arrived at the sleek, modern building that housed Emma's new workplace. The busy atmosphere of the office greeted them as they stepped inside, with colleagues hurrying about and the air abuzz with activity.

"Welcome to your new home away from home, Emma," her manager said with a reassuring smile as they made their way through the sea of desks.

Emma returned his smile, feeling a mixture of excitement and nerves at the prospect of starting her new job.

"Thanks, I'm excited to get started," she replied, her voice filled with determination.

Pierre remained by her side as Emma mingled among her new coworkers, graciously introducing her to each member of the team. Some greeted her with warm smiles and friendly gestures, while others seemed to regard her with more reserved expressions.

"Bonjour, Emma. It's a pleasure to have you join us," one colleague said, extending a hand in greeting.

"Likewise. I'm looking forward to working with you all," Emma replied, her tone friendly yet professional.

However, amidst the polite exchanges and introductions, Emma overheard a whispered conversation between two coworkers nearby. "I heard Pierre brought Emma in," one of them said, her voice tinged with curiosity. "It's strange, isn't it?

He's relatively new himself. Left a prestigious job in Milan to come here."

Emma's brows furrowed in surprise at the revelation, her mind buzzing with questions. Despite the nagging curiosity about Pierre's past, Emma knew she had more pressing matters to attend to. While her new job demanded her full attention, the excitement of exploring Paris awaited her outside the office walls.

As she settled into her new role, Emma found herself immersed in a whirlwind of meetings, presentations, and client interactions. With each passing day, she gained confidence in her abilities and formed stronger bonds with her colleagues, putting any lingering doubts about Pierre's background on the back burner.

A few weeks later, Emma received a special delivery at her new apartment. It was a thick envelope postmarked from home, and she immediately knew who it was from. Tearing it open with eager hands, Emma pulled out a sheaf of papers covered in Liam's familiar scrawl. Her heart swelled seeing his handwriting, feeling closer to him despite the distance.

"My dearest Emma," the letter began, and Emma's eyes scanned the pages eagerly as Liam poured his heart out.

He recounted their daily routines and shared his thoughts, expressing how proud he was of her accomplishments so far abroad. Each word felt like a warm embrace, comforting her and reminding her of their love.

Towards the end of the letter, Liam's words grew tender, expressing his longing for her presence.

"I miss your smile and the way you make me feel," he wrote, his love evident in every line.

Touched by Liam's heartfelt words and gesture, Emma felt tears prickling at the corners of her eyes. With a grateful heart, she reached for a pen and a sheet of paper, determined to convey her feelings in return. Pouring her love onto the page, Emma penned a handwritten letter of her own, expressing her gratitude, longing, and unwavering devotion to Liam.

In the following weeks, Emma and Liam continued exchanging handwritten letters, each one a precious treasure that bridged the distance between them.

Along with her letters, Emma sent small gifts from Paris. They served as tokens of her love and reminders of the adventures she was undertaking in her new home. Despite the miles that separated them, their love only grew stronger with each heartfelt exchange, a testament to the enduring power of their bond.

Chapter 10: Dancing in the Rain of Uncertainty

One busy afternoon, Liam sat at his desk, surrounded by the small gifts and postcards Emma had sent from Paris over the past few months. He ran his fingers gently over a miniature Eiffel Tower, one of the first gifts she had given to him when settling into Paris. Holding it now, he could almost picture her face lighting up at the landmark, eyes bright with excitement at the adventures awaiting her in her new home.

A small pang of longing arose in his chest. How he wished he could be there to experience it all alongside her, as they'd dreamed for so long. Instead, he was stuck here with only these mementos and her letters to carry him through her absence.

Setting the Eiffel Tower down, Liam picked up a postcard from the Louvre. In her messy scrawl, Emma had written how amazed she was by the artwork and said that she wished she could share it with him. A half-smile tugged at Liam's lips at the memory, but it quickly faded as worry crept back in.

Why had the letters and gifts suddenly stopped? For weeks now, he had received only vague texts in response to his messages, giving nothing away. It wasn't like Emma to leave him feeling so unsure and in the dark. He thought they would always tell each other everything, no matter how busy life got.

Liam chewed his lip anxiously, flipping the postcard over in his hands. His gut was screaming that something wasn't right, but he could not know what was going on without Emma willing to open up. All he had were these remnants of happier times and a growing pit of concern in his stomach.

"Everything alright, Liam?" asked Sarah, popping her head in. "You've been staring at that phone for ages."

Liam set it down with a frown.

"It's Emma. I haven't heard from her properly in weeks. Just these cursory little 'I'm fine' messages when I ask what's going on."

"Paris is a busy city. Lots going on at the new job, I'm sure," Sarah replied, leaning against the doorframe.

"Yeah, in her last message a few days ago, she said she was swamped with a project but would call soon. But now there's the radio silence, and it's worrying me," Liam sighed.

"This isn't like her. We tell each other everything," he added, picking up the postcard from the Eiffel Tower and tracing Emma's handwriting.

Sarah crossed her arms, regarding Liam thoughtfully.

"And this isn't like her at all, from what you've said. Emma's never been one to avoid your calls or leave you hanging," she said.

Nodding slowly, Liam leaned back in his chair.

"Do you think... is it silly of me to think something else could be going on? That maybe she's met someone there or is keeping something from me?" he asked, looking at Sarah, hopeful yet anxious for her opinion on the matter.

Sarah considered for a moment before responding.

"I don't think it's silly to have concerns, not with how she's been acting. But you know Emma - she wears her heart on her sleeve. If something was really going on, don't you think she would've said?"

"That's what I keep telling myself..." Liam said, running a hand through his hair. "I just need to talk to her properly. Figure out what's changed."

Sarah clapped a reassuring hand on his shoulder.

"Why don't you give her a call tonight, see if you can't get to the bottom of this, eh? I'm sure it's all just a big misunderstanding."

Liam smiled, grateful for Sarah's level-headed counsel.

"Yeah, you're right. No use worrying myself sick over maybes," he said, hoping a real conversation would finally set his mind at ease.

That evening, Liam headed home with a restless heart. He tried calling Emma, eager to catch her after work hours in Paris. But the phone only continued to ring, eventually going to voicemail.

"Emma, it's me. Please call back, I'm worried. I just... I need to know you're alright," Liam sighed heavily after leaving the message.

The unanswered call had only amplified his concerns. He paced down his flat, running scenarios through his head. What if she was in trouble and couldn't contact him? Or worse, what if she was purposely avoiding his calls?

He finally collapsed on the couch, staring at their last photos together before Emma left. Her smiling face used to bring him such joy but now only twisted his gut with unease. Liam knew he couldn't take the not-knowing much longer.

A plan started formulating in his mind. If Emma wouldn't answer his calls, he'd have to go to her in person. See with his own eyes that she was safe and hopefully get the truth about what was happening.

The next day, Liam took time off work and booked the earliest flight to Paris he could find. It was risky and impulsive, but he had to do something. He thought, come what may in Paris, at least he would have answers. He just prayed he wasn't already too late.

The next morning was a blur of activity as Liam packed a bag and raced to the airport. After what felt like the longest flight of his life, the plane finally descended into Paris.

As Liam gazed out the window, the city emerged in stunning detail. Patches of green and the glint of the Seine River snaked between tall buildings and grandiose architecture. It was a breathtaking sight, but one he had hoped to experience for the first time with Emma by his side.

When the aircraft doors opened, a rush of excitement and nerves coursed through Liam. He strode through the terminal with determination, taking in the bustle of travelers speaking in various languages. Signs pointed him to the Metro, and soon Liam found himself underground, zipping toward the heart of the city in a sleek railcar.

As he emerged on the ground again, Liam's breath caught at the iconic landmarks appearing one by one - Notre Dame, the Arc de Triomphe, the Champs-Elysées stretching ahead. It was everything he had seen in photos that came vibrantly to life.

But where was Emma in this dazzling cityscape?

Following the directions on his phone, Liam wove through winding streets, taking in charming cafes and stylish boutiques. Before long, he spotted Emma's apartment building rising above its neighbors. His heart pounded as he paused before buzzing her flat, hoping and praying she would answer. This was it - the moment of truth about what brought him all this way to Paris.

Liam checked the address on Emma's letters one last time before pressing the buzzer of her flat. He held his breath as it rang out, waiting to see her.

But although he anxiously waited for a response, none came. He pressed the button a few more times but to no avail. Doubts started creeping in as he rechecked the address.

Reaching for his phone with a sinking feeling, Liam called Emma's number. It rang endlessly before going to voicemail.

"Please pick up..." he muttered.

Emma finally answered on his third try.

"Liam? What's wrong?"

Quickly, Liam explained how he had come all this way only to find her apartment empty.

"Emma, where are you? I don't understand, I thought—"

"Liam, I'm so sorry. I should have told you, but things changed so fast..." she said, cutting him off gently.

As Emma explained being sent on a last-minute work trip to Nice, Liam sank onto the front steps in dismay. All his worries and fears came rushing back.

"I can't stay long in Paris," he said sadly. "I just had to see you to know you're alright."

"I know, and I would give anything to be there with you," Emma replied soothingly. "But this project is important. Just a few more days, and I'll be home, I promise."

Though disappointed, Liam took comfort in hearing her voice.

"A few days, then. Then we need to talk, Emma."

The flight back to San Francisco was bittersweet for Liam. Though Paris had lived up to its reputation as a charming city, leaving without Emma made it all feel rather hollow. Lost in thought, he barely noticed the hours pass as he gazed restlessly out the window. That is until a familiar voice jolted him from his reverie.

"Liam? Is that you?"

Turning, Liam broke into a smile, seeing Mark, his old college buddy.

"No way, what are the odds! How's it going, man?"

After exchanging greetings, Mark explained he'd just returned from a long work trip to New York.

"Crazy busy, but so much fun. Hey, want to grab a coffee when we land?"

Eager for a friendly distraction, Liam readily agreed. Once settled at the airport cafe, they caught up on the years since they had last met. As Liam and Mark chatted over coffee, it felt like old times had returned. They laughed, reminiscing about university hijinks and comparing how much had changed since.

Mark told tales of the big city grind in New York - long hours and crowded subways, but also amazing culture and energy.

"It's exhausting but never boring, that's for sure."

Liam, too, shared briefly about his business.

"Still feels surreal to call myself an entrepreneur sometimes."

"Hey, you've earned it. Still can't believe that you secured a mega deal with Chinese investors when you were still in your final year." Mark grinned. "Bet the Paris trip was successful, yeah? Any new business idea swirling around in that head of yours?"

Liam sighed.

"It... didn't quite work out as planned. But it's a beautiful city, no doubt filled with opportunities just waiting to be grabbed."

Not wanting to burden Mark with his romantic troubles, Liam steered the chat toward Mark's dating exploits in NYC. They laughed heartily at his string of, in Mark's words, "interesting characters." It felt cathartic for Liam to forget his worries for a while, bonding with an old friend. But soon, Mark would say something that flipped Liam's world upside down.

"Emma was in New York last week, can you believe it? Small world, right?" Mark said.

Liam felt his blood run cold at Mark's offhand comment. Emma in New York? It couldn't be true. He struggled to maintain an air of casual interest, hoping Mark wouldn't notice his rising panic.

"Emma, you say? In the big city?" Liam prayed his voice didn't betray the whirlwind of emotions within - panic, dread, confusion, and rising anger.

Mark, oblivious to Liam's internal turmoil, launched into the story. "Yeah, man, crazy right? I was at a mall and saw her across the room."

"Did you talk to her?" Liam asked.

"Nah, we couldn't meet. Before I could approach her, she had already left," Mark replied, shaking his head apologetically.

The sinking feeling in Liam's gut intensified. All he had was more questions and suspicions piling up.

"That's a shame," Liam replied, struggling to keep his tone light. "I flew all the way to Paris hoping to..."

He trailed off, lost in troubled thoughts. Emma's words from their phone call rang hollow in light of Mark's revelation. What else was she keeping from him?

The evening wore off, and Liam and Mark's conversation wound down. It was time to bid farewell. With a handshake and a promise to stay in touch, Liam and Mark parted ways.

***

The next few days passed in a blur for Liam as he recalled Mark's revelations over and over in his mind. He wanted so badly to believe Emma had a reasonable explanation for them. Yet doubts continued gnawing at him.

Liam threw himself into his work as a distraction, but it provided no solace as far as Emma's mysterious actions were concerned. He considered calling her, demanding the full truth once and for all. But fear of what he might discover held Liam back. The not-knowing tortured him, yet facing hard facts seemed like a greater agony.

Just as Liam was pacing restlessly around his flat on the third evening, his phone rang. When Emma's name appeared on Liam's phone, he took a steadying breath before answering.

"Emma. It's good to hear your voice."

"Hey, Liam. How have you been? I know we haven't talked since you visited me in Paris. I feel awful about it... I should have reached out sooner, but work has been crazy lately," Emma said, her tone sincere yet apologetic, leaving Liam even more confused. He didn't know what to believe anymore.

Liam hesitated for a moment, considering confronting Emma about what Mark had told him. But seeing her tired expression, he decided against it. If it wasn't true, he didn't want to hurt her further. Instead, he chose to engage her in conversation, hoping to lighten the mood.

"Hey, I understand work can be tough sometimes. No need to apologize," Liam said gently, reassuring her. "I've been missing you, though. Let me tell you about my experience in Paris."

Emma's tired eyes brightened a bit as Liam began sharing stories from his trip. He talked about the charming streets, the delicious food, and the breathtaking views. Her smile grew wider as he spoke, and for a moment, they both forgot about the tension lingering between them.

Although Liam still harbored doubts, talking to Emma made him feel as if everything was right in the world again. It was like the warmth of spring returning after a long, harsh winter. However, just as they were starting to reconnect, a sudden cold breeze swept through, withering the delicate flowers in the garden of their relationship.

It was early Friday evening, and Liam returned home with excitement bubbling inside him. He couldn't wait to call Emma and share all about his day when something shiny caught his eye. Placed among the usual stack of bills and flyers was a letter addressed to him with a sender marked only as "To Liam - 09765," Liam's college ID number.

His curiosity was piqued, and Liam furrowed his brow, wondering who could send him a letter using his old college ID.

Hesitantly, Liam picked up the letter and turned it over, searching for any clue about the sender. But to his surprise, there was no sender's name, adding an air of mystery to the situation. With a mix of anticipation and trepidation, Liam carried the letter inside and settled onto the couch, the weight of it heavy in his hands.

Carefully, he tore open the envelope and unfolded the letter inside. As he read the words on the page, his heart sank, and his world seemed to come crashing down around him. The letter contained a secret about Emma, one that she had kept hidden, believing no one would ever discover it.

As Liam read on, the truth unfolded before him, shattering the image he had of Emma and leaving him grappling with a whirlwind of emotions. Shock, disbelief, and betrayal washed over him in waves as he struggled to come to terms with what he had just learned.

For a moment, Liam sat there in stunned silence, the weight of the revelation pressing down on him like a leaden weight. Everything he thought he knew about Emma was called into question, leaving him reeling and uncertain about what to do next.

Slowly, the reality of the situation began to sink in, and Liam felt a deep sense of loss wash over him. The future he had envisioned with Emma, the plans they had made, all now seemed uncertain and fragile.

With a heavy heart, Liam realized everything would change between him and Emma. The foundation of trust they had built, now cracked and crumbling, threatened to tear them apart. But amidst the pain and confusion, one thing remained clear: he needed to confront Emma and seek the truth, no matter how painful it was.

www.ingramcontent.com/pod-product-compliance
Lightning Source LLC
Chambersburg PA
CBHW061239140726
47998CB00006B/2042